Chicke

D1077305

Chicken

ALAN GIBBONS

Illustrations by Derek Brazell

A Dolphin
Paperback

To Joe Long

First published in Great Britain by
Dent Children's Books in 1993
Printed in paperback in 1994
by Orion Children's Books
a division of the Orion Publishing Group Ltd
Orion House
5 Upper St Martin's Lane
London WC2H 9EA

Text copyright © Alan Gibbons 1993
Illustrations copyright © Derek Brazell 1993

Printed in England by Clays Ltd, St Ives plc

A catalogue record for this book is available from
the British Library

ISBN 1 85881 051 5

Contents

CHAPTER ONE
Webbo

'Are you walking up to the gate, Davy?' asked Craig as we reached the classroom door.

'No,' I replied, 'I've got to pick up The Mouth.'

Craig pulled a suitable face. The Mouth is my little sister Anna. Anna is to talking what Krakatoa was to volcanoes. She stopped talking once and everybody thought they'd gone deaf.

'I'll bring in my ollies tomorrow,' said Craig. 'I've got half a dozen new meatheads. 'See you.'

'See you,' I mumbled. I didn't like to tell him that I wasn't interested in marbles. In fact, as I came in sight of Webbo lolling against the wall, marbles couldn't have been further from my thoughts. I was interested in Webbo, though. I had to be; he'd become one of the most important people in my life, and I wasn't a bit happy about it. I waited for the inevitable put-down, but for once, he didn't have anything to say, and confined himself to a superior smirk as I edged past him. When it comes to smiling, Webbo's in the Jaws league.

'Oh, Davy,' said Craig, turning round, 'What did your mum say about the disco?'

'She says I've got to go,' I said, in the most grudging and unenthusiastic voice I could muster. 'Anna wants to go to

1

the Infant one, so I've got to go to the Juniors. Wonderful, isn't it? Held to ransom by a five-year-old! What idiot ever dreamed up the idea of a school disco anyway?

The infants run wild and throw up on the teachers, at least that's what I did when I was an infant. Then it's the juniors' turn. The lads try to act cool and the girls raid their mums' make-up kits. No, discos just didn't suit me at all.

'Oh, cheer up,' grinned Craig. 'It'll be a laugh.'

Sure, but at whose expense?

I still wonder how I came to make friends with Craig. He loves football. Liverpool FC isn't just his team, it's his religion. As for me, I couldn't tell an Arsenal from an Accrington Stanley. What's more, Craig is popular with everyone. He even got on with Webbo until I arrived. I'd become a bit of a loner since moving school.

I poked my nose out of the classroom door. It was an April afternoon, but it looked more like November. Spring hadn't so much sprung, as sprung a leak. I'd never seen rain like it. It came drifting in grey waves across the playground. As I hurried round the corner of the building towards the Infants, I cast a wary glance over my shoulder. It was all right, Webbo wasn't following. He'd been like a second shadow all week, but worse – shadows don't shove you around. Mind you, today had been better than most. He hadn't called me names, or thumped me.

'Hello, Davy,' said Mrs Collins, as I reached the Reception class. 'Anna's over there, talking to Rebecca.'

Talking; it figured. Birds fly, fish swim and Anna talks. It's her natural state.

'Come on, Anna,' I called impatiently. 'Mum will be waiting for us at the gate and it's pouring.'

'I saw a goat,' said Anna as she took my hand.

'Big deal,' I answered shortly. 'It was a trip to the farm, wasn't it? If you go to a farm, it's odds-on you'll see a goat.'

2

Now what did I say that for? I made a belated attempt at sounding interested. 'You were lucky you missed all this rain.'

'Goats smell,' said Anna, wrinkling her nose and dismissing my interest with the contempt it probably deserved. 'The big white one was the worst. He smelt worse that Dad's socks.'

'Don't let Dad hear you say that,' I warned.

'I've got something too,' whispered Anna, looking around furtively.

'What, sweets or something?'

'No,' chuckled Anna, 'Not sweets. This is better than sweets.'

I could see that she was bursting to tell somebody, but I didn't find out until later just what Anna did have. Webbo saw to that.

'Not another Woollyback!' he scoffed. 'Isn't one enough? I thought I told you, Davy, this is a Scouse-only school.'

Put another record on, I've heard it all before, is what I thought.

'This is Anna,' is what I said.

Anna stared at Webbo curiously. I just hoped The Mouth wasn't going to talk me into even more bother. Luckily, Mum arrived before Anna managed to drop me in it. She was jogging down the path from the school gates with an umbrella. 'Get under this, you two,' she ordered. 'You're going to catch your deaths.'

'See you, Woolly,' sneered Webbo.

I hated him from the top of his flat head to the soles of his Reebok trainers. I shivered at the cold, stinging rain. Webbo and the downpour; they both made me feel grim.

'Did you have a nice day, love?' asked Mum, as Anna scrambled for a hug. 'Did you do all your work, Davy?'

Typical. To Anna it's *Did you have a nice day?* But does

3

she say the same to me? Oh no, sometime between starting school and going into the Juniors it changes to *Did you do all your work?* Well, yes, as a matter of fact I had done all my work. I'd drawn a Tudor theatre, completed two pages of my maths book, and written a poem all about Spring. In my poem it was sunny and lambs danced among the falling apple blossom; in the playground it was lashing with rain and the only thing I saw dancing all afternoon was Jimmy Owens, when he wanted to use the toilet.

'Are you all right, Davy?' asked Mum, fighting to make herself heard over The Mouth's edited highlights of *My Day at the Farm.*

'Yes, Mum, I'm all right.'

'The man let me hold a rabbit,' chattered Anna. 'Can we have a rabbit? I'll feed it, and clean its cage . . .'

'Hutch,' I interrupted, as we turned into Talbot Avenue.

'What?'

'Hutch,' I repeated. 'A rabbit lives in a hutch, not a cage.'

'This rabbit was in a cage,' retorted Anna. 'It was a big one and there were hundreds of rabbits in it.'

'Hundreds!' I sniggered.

'Oh, don't spoil it for Anna,' said Mum, 'What's up with you today? You're really grumpy.'

I shrugged my shoulders and stamped through a puddle.

'Shall I take your school bag, Anna?' asked Mum.

'No!' cried Anna. 'I want to carry it.'

'OK, love,' said Mum, taken aback by Anna's abrupt reply. Normally, she was only too happy to let Mum take her bag. 'Anyway, go on, Anna,' continued Mum. 'What else did you see at the farm?'

'Anna brought something back,' I yawned absent-mindedly, earning a ferocious glare from my little sister.

4

'Did you?' asked Mum. 'What is it?'

Anna's mouth was hanging open. She closed it for a moment, then opened it again. She looked like a startled codfish.

'I never!' she yelled.

'I thought . . .'

'I never!' insisted Anna, clenching her fists until the knuckles turned white.

'OK, OK,' I sighed, holding up my hands in a gesture of surrender. 'I must have misunderstood. I'm sorry.' I was surprised by the force of Anna's denial. Whatever it was she'd hinted at was obviously a state secret.

'Well,' Mum observed. 'You two have come out of school in a fine old mood, I must say.'

What did she expect? School these days was worse than the measles. The trouble was, there was no cure, at least not for the next six or eight years.

By now, Anna had recovered sufficiently from the shock of me mentioning The Something She Had Brought Back, to gabble on about the farm. I switched off; my memory didn't though. It would have been bad enough having to put up with Webbo at school, but I couldn't leave him behind, he had got right inside my head. Why me? Why had he taken such an instant dislike to me?

The term's first rounders match had got me off to a bad start, of course. I remember Webbo yelling 'Get it!'. Well, how was I to know Lianne Whalley would sky the ball straight at me just when I was busy watching the seagulls pecking the leftover crisps off the Infants' yard? I didn't ask to be in the vital place at the last match-deciding moment. Five rounders each and only my hands between victory and defeat.

'Catch the thing!' bawled Webbo as he raced towards me. I didn't, of course. I tried. I stuck out my hands and did my best to cup them under the ball. I suppose my big

5

chance to be a hero was just too much for me. I closed my eyes and hoped for the best, but the ball popped out of my hands as easily as it had dropped in. Lianne completed the rounder with her arms raised in triumph, while Pete Moran laughed himself sick at my attempt at a catch. Webbo wasn't laughing. He only played to win, and I'd just scuppered his hopes. Webbo didn't like being on the losing side – *ever*.

'You,' hissed Webbo, prodding a finger into my chest. 'You are dead.'

No, he definitely did not like being on the losing side. I looked around. Nobody was listening, nobody except Craig, and he just grimaced sympathetically.

'Try to keep out of Webbo's way,' he advised on the way back into school.

That was easier said than done. I'd realized on my first day since the move from Yorkshire a few months back that Webbo and I weren't going to get on.

'Hey, Woollyback,' he had shouted in the playground.

I must have looked blank.

'Yes, you,' he said. 'Don't you know what a Woolly-back is?'

I shook my head. That was a mistake.

'Well, soft lad,' explained Webbo. 'It's like this. There are two kinds of people in the world, Scousers and Woollybacks. If you don't come from Liverpool, then you're a Woollyback. You're not from Liverpool, are you?'

No, I wasn't. I'd finally discovered that I had something in common with Michael Jackson, Arnold Schwarzenegger, the Pope and Mother Theresa of Calcutta – we're all Woollybacks!

'So now you understand, don't you, Woollyback?'

I nodded and turned to walk away. Carl O'Rourke barred my way.

6

'Who said you could go?' demanded Webbo.

'Nobody,' I admitted. Silly me, I didn't know I needed permission!

'Then you wait till you're told you can go,' said Webbo. 'Understand?'

'Yes,' I murmured nervously. 'I understand.'

'Hear that?' announced Webbo to Carl and his other mate, Vinny Boyle. 'This Woollyback understands Scouse. It looks like we won't need that interpreter after all.'

Vinny and Carl sneered. I managed a thin smile.

'Off you go then, Woolly,' ordered Webbo.

I turned to go, but Webbo took my leg from under me with a trip. I sprawled full-length on the playground skinning my elbow, setting off hoots of laughter behind me.

'Clumsy aren't they, these Woollybacks?' snorted Vinny.

'It's living up hills that does it,' said Webbo. 'It makes their feet a funny shape.'

I turned my funny-shaped feet towards the classroom and vowed to stay out of Webbo's way. Unfortunately, in a school the size of Bride Lane that was easier said than done. I've seen sardine tins that are less cramped.

'A penny for them,' said Mum, as we reached the front gate.

Her voice wrenched me out of my gloomy thoughts. 'What?'

'You mean "pardon," ' corrected Mum. Once in a while, she would get on her high horse about talking properly. By the time she'd reminded me to say "pardon" instead of "what", I'd forgotten what she wanted in the first place.

'What?' I repeated lamely.

'Stop saying "what" all the time,' said Mum. She was getting exasperated. 'I was checking whether you were still with us. You've been really quiet. Are you sure you're all right?'

'Of course I'm sure,' I snapped. 'Just because our Anna never shuts up, it doesn't mean I have to be the same.'

'Pardon me for breathing,' said Mum.

The moment she opened the front door Anna bolted up the stairs. She was up to something all right, but I felt too downright weary to find out what.

CHAPTER TWO
Feeding Time

Tea-time in our house is worse than a chimpanzees' tea party, and that Thursday night we were two chimps short. Dad was still at work, and Anna was upstairs with The Something She Had Brought Back.

'What's Anna doing?' asked Mum.

'She's playing in her room,' I replied diplomatically.

'Anna?' gasped Mum. '*Our* Anna? She never plays upstairs.'

'She is tonight,' I said.

'Well, will somebody go and get her?' asked Mum, scattering cutlery on the table. 'Go on, Colin, you're not doing anything.'

I looked up from my computer game and squinted expectantly at Colin.

'Davy'll go,' grunted Colin. I could see he was busy lounging on the couch and all I had to do was while away the time with a really exciting computer game! I glared at him and stamped upstairs, wondering why older brothers are such creeps.

'Who's that?' yelled Anna as I arrived outside her door.

'It's me,' I answered.

'Stay!' she commanded.

Stay? What did she think I was, an Alsatian puppy?

'Well?' asked Anna, easing the door open a crack,

9

'What do you want?'

I tried to steal a glance at The Something She Had Brought Back, but it was no use. Anna was blocking the way; she'd make a great bouncer. She'd thought better of letting me in on her secret.

'Tea's ready,' I explained.

'Oh!' growled Anna, closing the door. 'Hang on, I won't be a minute.'

As I waited on the landing, I could hear a scrabbling and a scratching, then a scraping and a shuffling. Finally, Anna slid out of the barely-open door.

'What have you got in there?' I asked.

'Mind your own business,' said Anna. 'Beat you downstairs.'

'Where's my tea?' grumbled Colin, slithering off the couch and padding across the living room in his stockinged feet. 'I'm going out.'

'Out where?' asked Mum suspiciously.

'Just out,' said Colin.

'Who with?'

'Mates.'

'Which mates?' demanded Mum, as she began depositing plates on the table.

'You know,' said Colin, 'Lads off the estate.'

'Am I talking English?' asked Mum, glancing at me for support.

'You are,' I confirmed. 'Colin isn't.' She ought to have known by now that our Colin communicates by a series of grunts. One grunt for food, two for money, and that's about it.

'Oh, where's your dad?' Mum asked nobody in particular. 'I've got to get to work.'

Dad usually got in about half past five, and Mum had to be out by a quarter to six to catch her bus. She worked for a couple of hours an evening cleaning offices in town. It

10

was always a close-run thing getting out in time, and Mum got more ill-tempered as the clock ticked round to a quarter to six.

'He'll make it,' said Colin. 'He always does.'

Colin's laid-back like Dad. I take after Mum; I worry about everything there is to worry about and then some.

'What's this?' asked Colin, poking at his tea with his fork.

'Lasagne,' said Mum.

'It looks like a dog-food butty,' complained Colin. 'Didn't you do any chips?'

'Eat it,' said Mum. 'It'll do you good.'

'I'd rather have chips,' said Colin.

'One more word and I'll give your tea to the cat,' warned Mum.

'Oh, so it's a cat-food butty,' quipped Colin.

The last remark broke the tension a bit. Even Mum had to smile. I looked at her. She was really worried about Colin. The estate wasn't a bit like the pit village where we grew up. The traffic was terrible and there were kids hanging about on the street corners until late in the evening. Mum thought it was shocking. Dad always said it wasn't that bad, but we all knew he hated it too. We'd had to move to Liverpool when he got a job maintaining lifts. He'd been delighted at first. He'd almost given up hope of ever getting a job after the pit closed. The trouble was, the money wasn't much good. So here we were stuck on a run-down housing estate on the edge of the city without two pennies to rub together.

'Right,' said Colin, gulping down the last mouthful of cat-food butty, 'I'm off out.'

'Take care,' called Mum, 'And don't stay out late.'

The back door slammed. He didn't even manage a grunt this time.

'Where *has* your dad got to?' fumed Mum. 'It's gone

twenty to. If he rolls up late, I'll go mad. Doesn't he understand that we need my wage to pay the bills . . . ?'

She was cut off in mid-rant by the sound of the car pulling into the driveway.

'About time,' she complained, flying past Dad through the open door.

'Yes,' sniped Dad. 'I have had a nice day.'

'You should get home earlier,' called Mum, as she set off down the street. 'I hate having to run for the bus.'

'You wouldn't need to if you passed your driving test,' retorted Dad, as she disappeared round the corner.

I hated them quarrelling. It had never been like this back in Yorkshire, but ever since the pit closed there had been all sorts of rows. Mum thought it was a mistake to take such a poorly-paid job, and Dad felt guilty about taking us away from the village where we'd all been so happy.

'Dad!' squealed Anna, glad of an excuse to leave the lasagne half-eaten.

'Hi there, pigeon,' he said, beaming at the attention. 'Where's Colin?'

'Out with his mates,' I replied.

'That's where you should be,' said Dad. 'It isn't healthy for a lad of your age to be hanging round the house.'

Here we go, I thought, another lecture about getting out and making some friends.

'You need to get out like our Colin,' continued Dad. 'He's making new friends. All you do is mope around the house with your nose stuck in a book.'

Mope! I did not mope. I enjoyed my own company, what on earth was wrong with that?

'Anyway, what's for tea.'

'Cat-food butty,' giggled Anna.

'You what?'

'Cat-food butty.'

'Let's have a butchers,' said Dad, walking into the kitchen. 'Good God, it is too!'

'It's lasagne,' I explained. We'd had it before lots of times. Why did everybody make such a fuss every time we had something more adventurous than egg and chips?

'I think I'll swop with Flapjack,' said Dad. 'Do you fancy this, old son?'

Flapjack blinked at him, then carried on licking his paws.

'No, I don't blame you,' sighed Dad.

'Oh, give it a rest, Dad,' I complained. 'It's nice. Why do you always do this?'

'What's got into you?' demanded Dad. 'It's only a joke.'

'Sure,' I muttered. 'Only a joke.'

'Oh, cheer up Davy,' said Dad, 'It'll never happen.'

It already had.

'I went to the farm today,' chirped Anna.

'Did you, love?' asked Dad. 'Come over here and tell me all about it.'

That was the signal for me to retreat to my room. I pulled out a book of Viking legends and began to leaf through it. Somewhere between Loki and Thor the Thunder God, I realized that my mind was straying. I was preoccupied with Webbo. I rose and walked over to the window to give myself something else to think about. From there, I could see the patch of waste ground where Colin spent most of his time just lately.

Sure enough, there he was on his new mountain bike, looking laid-back and talking to the lads from round the corner in Cromwell Avenue. I looked admiringly at the bike. It was his thirteenth birthday present. Colin reckoned it must have cost a cool £150. For some reason, I remained at the window watching them. I expected something to happen, and it did. A sapphire blue Sierra accelerated up from Queen's Drive. I watched the Sierra,

13

then glanced back at Colin's group. One of the older boys, Ricky Scholes had detached himself from the others and was pedalling his bike to the top of the mound which overlooked the main road. There was no mistaking his intentions. Ricky waited until the Sierra was almost on top of him then rode furiously down the slope. My heart leapt as he bumped across the road in front of the car.

'You young idiot!' yelled the driver as he slammed on the brakes, sending up a puff of black tyre-smoke.

Ricky didn't even look round. Instead he rode on, cackling in triumph at his show of bravado. He punched the air as if he'd just scored the winner in the World Cup Final.

I leaned my forehead against the window, feeling it cold and damp on my skin. 'I hope you know what you're doing, Col,' I murmured. 'I just hope you know what you're doing.'

I'd always looked up to Colin, but just lately he'd been acting like a real idiot. I think he missed his old mates. He seemed prepared to do anything to make new ones.

'You up there, Davy?' called Dad from the bottom of the stairs.

'Yes.'

'I'm just giving Anna her bath, OK?'

I heard dad and Anna climbing the stairs and poked my head out.

'Do you want something, Davy?' asked Dad.

'No,' I replied. 'Not really.'

I did want something. I wanted to tell him what Colin was getting himself into, but I let it pass. After all, I couldn't see Dad taking any notice. He had enough on his plate.

'Did you hear something?' he asked as he passed Anna's room.

'No,' said Anna.

Dad frowned. 'I'm sure I heard something scratching,'

he said. 'Yes, there it goes again. You heard it, didn't you, Davy?'

Anna looked at me with wide, appealing eyes. She needn't have worried; my mind was elsewhere.

'Oh well,' said Dad. 'Let's get this bath run, Anna.'

Suddenly there was a knock at the front door.

'Oh, what now?' grumbled Dad.

I watched him run downstairs, and winked at Anna. She gave me a broad smile. I was just about feeling good when I heard the news which cast a dark shadow over the whole evening.

'Is Davy in, Mr Watts?' came a woman's voice. 'I'm Craig's mum. He's had a bit of an accident. Oh, there you are Davy.'

'Is he all right?' asked Dad, as I joined him at the front door.

'Oh, he'll live,' said Mrs Morgan. 'He was jumping off the chest of drawers on to his bed. Unfortunately, he missed. He's cut his lip and cracked a couple of teeth. I've got to take him to the dentist in the morning. Will you give this note to Mr Clarke, Davy?'

I took the note. 'Is he still going to the disco?' I asked.

'I very much doubt it,' said Mrs Morgan. 'He's got lips like rubber tyres at the moment.'

I watched her walk off down the street. The disco would have been bad enough with Craig. Without him, it was going to be a nightmare. Maybe I ought to take a dive off the chest of drawers too!

CHAPTER THREE

Teaching Fish to Swim

'No,' said Mum. 'You are not giving me a driving lesson and that's final. 'I've just spent an hour cleaning floors.'

Colin glanced at me and rolled his eyes. This nightly ritual bored him as much as it did me. 'I think I'll go back out,' he said.

'Oh no you don't,' said Mum.

'You can't tie him to your apron strings, Sandra,' said Dad. That was getting to be his favourite phrase.

'I don't want to,' sighed Mum, 'But I do want to know where he is.'

'Fair enough,' said Dad. 'Let's go for a run in the car like I suggested. That way, you'll know exactly where he is.'

Mum pursed her lips. She'd painted herself into a corner. 'All right then. But be patient.'

'Patience,' exclaimed Dad, 'is my middle name.'

Oh yeah, and mine was Tinkerbell! It was Mum's turn to roll her eyes. Asking Dad to teach someone to drive was like asking Frankenstein to teach ballet.

'Anna,' called Mum. 'Get your coat, love. We're going out.'

No answer. 'Anna! Did you hear me?'

The bedroom door creaked open. 'What do you want, Mum?' asked Anna.

16

'Your dad wants us to go out in the car.' Mum ran her fingers through her hair. She always fiddles with her hair when she's nervous.

'Where?'

'For a run, that's all.'

'Oh, you're not learning to drive again, are you?' groaned Anna.

'And what's wrong with that?' demanded Mum. 'I've only failed my test once, you know.'

'Is Dad going to shout at you again?' Anna asked.

Mum gave Dad a sidelong glance. 'He'd better not,' she warned.

Dad wore his most innocent expression: 'What, me shout? Never!'

'What's Anna up to anyway?' asked Colin. 'I've never known her to spend so much time in her room.'

Mum frowned. 'I've been wondering about that.'

'Ready?' asked Dad, dangling the keys in front of Mum.

'I suppose so.' Mum reluctantly took the keys.

We hadn't even got as far as Stanley Park before Dad started. 'Not so heavy on the brakes! You'll put the examiner through the windscreen like that. Easy, easy.'

'I told you Dad was going to shout,' said Anna.

Colin nodded and looked out of the window at Everton's ground. 'Do you think we'll get tickets for the Derby match, Dad?' he asked.

'No problem,' Dad replied. 'Oh, for God's sake, Sandra, you can't stay in third all the way. Change up, change *up*.'

Mum heaved a deep sigh; she was getting fed up.

'Can we go somewhere?' asked Anna.

'How's about Timbuctoo?' suggested Dad.

'No, I'd rather have Timbucthree,' drawled Colin.

'Where did you get that one?' I asked. '*Beano* annual 1955 or something?'

'1955,' Mum murmured. 'That's the year I was born.'

'Did they have cars then?' asked Anna.

Colin burst out laughing. 'Yes, but they had to walk in front with a red flag.'

'Shut up, you,' warned Mum. 'How about the Albert Dock?'

'Yes,' agreed Dad. 'We can watch the ferry if it runs at this time.'

'But why did they have a red flag?' asked Anna, setting Colin off again.

'Hand brake!' barked Dad, as Mum pulled up and unclipped her seat belt. 'Always put the hand brake on.'

'Oh, put it on yourself,' shouted Mum, storming off.

'What did I say?' Dad asked, all innocent. 'What did I say?'

'Beats me,' replied Colin.

I shook my head and jogged after Mum as she marched towards Mann Island. As I caught up with her, I could still hear Anna asking: 'But what's the red flag for?'

'Your dad can be a real pain in the neck sometimes,' said Mum.

'He doesn't mean anything,' I said. It was true; he didn't. He'd always been a great father until the move to Liverpool. He used to take us out all the time. We knew that nothing mattered to him more than we did. I felt torn. I loved the dad he used to be and wanted him back.

I turned round. Dad and Colin were swinging Anna between them along the pavement. They'd found a way to make her forget about the red flag.

'Is there anything wrong, Davy?' mum asked, as we reached the railings overlooking the river.

I shrugged my shoulders.

'I didn't hear you say no.'

18

'No,' I answered dully. 'Nothing's wrong.'

'Are you sure? I thought you were happier since you and Craig became mates.'

'Yes, Craig's all right.'

'So why all the long faces? Is it the work?'

'Mum,' I said, 'I'm all right.'

'Am I supposed to say sorry?' asked Dad, saving me from further grilling.

Mum tossed her auburn hair stubbornly.

'I'm sorry,' said Dad. 'Look, this is me being sorry.' He got down on his knees, and pointed to his chin. 'Here, hit me. Go on, hit me.'

That's my dad; always the clown.

'Come on, hit me,' he repeated, holding out his hands. Mum didn't, but Anna did, hard enough to make him flinch.

'Serves you right,' said Mum, permitting herself a smile as Dad rubbed his smarting nose.

'Are you driving back?' asked Dad.

'No way,' said Mum.

'Oh, come on, Sandra,' he pleaded. 'How can I teach you to drive if you bottle out all the time?'

'Come off it, Ray,' retorted Mum. 'You couldn't teach a fish to swim.'

'Who was that?' asked Mum as she opened the front door.

'Who?'

'You know who; the boy who waved to you back there.'

'Oh, you mean Ricky,' said Colin, dismissively.

'Ricky who?'

Colin frowned and looked away.

I provided the information instead. 'Scholes, Ricky Scholes.'

'Scholes?' said Mum. 'They're the ones from round the

corner, aren't they? Always in trouble with the police.'

'Search me,' said Colin, making his way inside.

'Anna love, do you want me to read you a story?' asked Dad. I think he was keen to avoid a quarrel. Mum was on a short fuse after the driving lesson.

'No thanks,' replied Anna, climbing the stairs. 'I think I'll go straight to bed.'

'Did she volunteer to go to bed?' gasped Mum, quite forgetting to pursue the matter of Ricky Scholes with Colin.

'Yes,' answered Dad. He looked shocked.

'Perhaps I'd better look in on her,' said Mum. 'You don't think she's coming down with something, do you?'

'Leave her, Sand,' said Dad. 'She just wants a bit of time to herself, that's all.'

Mum hesitated, then smiled. 'Yes, I suppose she's got a lot to put up with.'

'You don't mean us, do you?' protested Colin.

'Not us,' I said. 'You.'

'I can still batter you, you know,' warned Colin, only half-joking.

'Is that the sort of talk you hear from Ricky Scholes?' asked Mum.

'Leave it, Sandra,' advised Dad.

Mum did leave it, but only until Colin, Anna and I were safely in bed. I could hear her and Dad arguing until well after ten. They took their usual corners. Dad in the blue, insisting that Colin had to make new friends, and he couldn't do that stuck in the house like me. Mum in the red, equally convinced that Colin would only get into trouble hanging around with the likes of Ricky Scholes. I must have dozed off soon afterwards, but woke again around midnight. I could hear Anna's door creaking.

If I wanted to discover her secret, this seemed as good a time as any.

'Anna!' I exclaimed, discovering her sneaking back into her room. 'What are you—?'

'Sh!' she hissed.

I watched her door close. That's when it hit me. She'd been carrying Flapjack's red litter-tray.

CHAPTER FOUR
Woolly the Wimp

'It was here last night,' insisted Mum.

'Must've been burglars,' chuckled Dad.

'Very funny. Take a look for yourself if you don't believe me. It's gone.'

'It'll be in all the papers,' Dad went on wryly. '*Cat litter stolen – Police are looking for a very small thief with whiskers.* Hey, you don't think somebody crawled in through the cat flap, do you?'

'It must have been a cat burglar,' added Colin.

Mum was not amused. 'Do you know anything about this, Colin?'

'Why me?'

'Don't look at me, Mum,' I said. I meant it too. Don't look at me or I might just give Anna away.

'What about you, Anna?' asked Mum.

Anna shook her head then carried on shovelling her cornflakes. The Mouth did enjoy her meals from time to time, especially when a careless word might give the game away. So long as her jaws were occupied munching cornflakes, Anna was safe.

'I'll have a good look for it tonight,' said Mum. 'I said I'd go into Anna's class today to help Mrs Collins, so there's no time now.'

'What do you do when you go into school?' asked Dad.

'All sorts,' said Mum. 'Last week we were growing cress in egg shells.'

'Hell's teeth!' cried Dad suddenly. 'Have you seen the time?'

Dad's exclamation was the signal for a frantic burst of activity. I seized the opportunity to lean across to Anna.

'What *is* the cat litter for?'

Anna wasn't saying. I may have covered for her, but it obviously didn't entitle me to be let in on her big secret.

'Now,' said Mum as Dad hurried up the path to the car, 'have you got your packed lunch, Davy?'

I nodded.

'Anna, have you got your reading book?'

Anna nodded.

'I'm sure I've forgotten something,' said Mum.

'You have,' I told her, doing my best to suppress a giggle. 'You're still wearing your slippers.'

As we walked to school the happiness I'd felt over breakfast time began to fade. The smallest of grey clouds started to form in my mind. Its name was Webbo. I made a mental list of all the good and bad things which lay ahead of me. Being one of those people who likes to get the worst out of the way first, I started with the bad things.

Bad things:
Webbo,
Webbo's mates,
No Craig
School disco.

Good things:
Like all days, it was bound to end sometime.

I watched Anna teasing the dogs in Talbot Avenue. The

23

grey cloud now filled the sky. All I could think about was Webbo and what he had in store for me, and occasionally the disco, and how I was going to squirm with embarrassment the whole evening.

'Have a nice day, Davy,' said Mum as we walked through the school gates. My face must have given me away, because Mum immediately added: 'Are you quite sure nothing's wrong?'

'I've told you, haven't I?' I replied grudgingly.

'Have you? I wonder why I don't believe you.'

I shrugged my shoulders, tousled Anna's dark-blonde hair and jogged towards the classroom. I wasn't at all sure which was worse; Webbo's tormenting, or mum nagging me.

'Here's the Woollyback,' came Webbo's mocking voice. It went right through me, filling me with apprehension. Vinny Boyle was with him. Craig said Vinny had the IQ of a lettuce, but I think that's unfair to lettuces.

'What's your name again, Woolly?' asked Webbo.

This was a new routine. Vinny was already grinning in expectation.

'You know my name, Webbo,' I said. I winced. The words had come out sounding braver than I'd intended. I was scared stiff and certainly didn't mean to provoke him.

'It's slipped my mind,' continued Webbo, winking at Vinny. 'What was it now? Witts, Wetts . . .'

'Watts,' I said wearily.

'What?' demanded Webbo.

'Watts,' I repeated, but even I heard my voice catch.
'What?'

So that was it. They had lousy taste in jokes but I wasn't going to say so. They didn't need much of an excuse to turn really nasty. Instead, I kept my mouth firmly shut and tried to push past.

24

'You're a real wimp, Woolly,' sneered Vinny. Gone was the taunting mockery. It was replaced by something harsher and much more threatening.

'Yes,' cackled Webbo, 'That's him all right, Woolly the Wimp.'

I gave a long sigh. The moment I heard it I realized it was a nickname that was going to stick.

'That's a good one,' said Vinny, full of admiration at Webbo's inventiveness. 'Woolly the Wimp. I like it.'

I succeeded in reaching the classroom door and leaned against it, heart thumping, waiting impatiently for Mr Clarke to arrive and give me sanctuary.

'Hey, Carl,' shouted Vinny, as the third member of the gang arrived. 'Have you heard what Webbo just called the Woollyback?'

'What?'

'Woolly the Wimp. Good, isn't it?'

Carl snorted with amusement. He sounded for all the world like a happy pig.

'Woolly the Wimp? Oh, that's him all right. Did you hear that, Woolly? Woolly the Wimp.'

I'd heard it all right, but I held my tongue. I had no intention of tossing petrol on to the flames. Tears were already stinging my eyes and I pressed my face against the door jamb to hide how much they'd got to me. To my relief, I heard the security lock turn and stepped back from the door. Mr Clarke was opening up, and about time too. Hardly had I taken a step into the classroom than I felt a stinging sensation on the back of my neck.

Instinctively, I turned only to see Webbo twisting an elastic band round his finger.

'Aw, did that hurt?' he scoffed.

I lowered my eyes. Deep inside, I was boiling with anger and frustration, but I didn't dare let it show. I just stood there, feeling miserable.

'What a wimp,' observed Carl.

'Yes,' said Vinny, revelling in my discomfort. 'Woolly the Wimp.'

Mr Clarke shook his head as he read the note from Craig's mum. 'Trust Craig,' he murmured. 'Fancy landing on his face.'

'Fell on his face,' chortled Vinny as he brushed past. 'What a divvy.'

I managed not to turn this time. I'd made my mind up that it was best not to even look at my three tormentors. The moment you rose to one of their jibes, they'd won.

'What a pair of wimps,' said Webbo out of Mr Clarke's hearing. 'Taking the day off for a cut lip. He's nearly as bad as the Woollyback.'

My neck burned where he had flicked me with the elastic band. It was as if the mark became the place where every insult gathered, reminding me of the sharp, stinging pain, and all the sharp, stinging pains to come.

'Settle down,' said Mr Clarke, darting a warning glance in Webbo's direction. 'I'm going to take the register.'

As I waited for my name to be called, the atmosphere in the room became stifling. The grey cloud filled the whole classroom. Soon it would fill the whole world.

'Davy Watts,' called Mr Clarke.

'What?' shouted Webbo, repeating his stupid joke.

This time I couldn't help myself. Doing my best to hide the tears of humiliation in my eyes, I glanced round to see him cupping a hand behind his ear as if he were deaf.

'Here, Mr Clarke,' I replied, somehow disguising the hurt I was feeling.

'John Webster,' called Mr Clarke, frowning at Webbo's interruption.

'Here,' yawned Webbo.

'Here what?'

'Here, Mr Clarke,' said Webbo, pulling a face.

'Right,' said Mr Clarke, closing his register. 'Get out your writing books, Year Six.'

I pulled out my drawer, and stared helplessly at my book. There on the cover was the freshly-scrawled message: *This book belongs to Woolly the Wimp.*

CHAPTER FIVE
Smacked lunch

'Just before you go for your dinner break,' said Mr Clarke, 'I've a little announcement.'

A few of the kids pulled faces apprehensively.

'You're going to like this,' he continued, after a short pause to allow the fidgeting to stop. 'And that's an order.'

I think that was meant as a joke, but nobody laughed.

'You may remember your dance lessons with Mrs Ball,' he continued, provoking loud groans from the back of the room.

'We called her Ballroom Ball,' Tony Gordon told me in a whisper. 'She made us do barn dancing.'

'Good job she retired,' added Lee Phillips. 'She was cracking us up.'

'Well,' Mr Clarke went on, 'As we haven't done much dance this term, I've invited one of the teachers from the college to come in next week and take you for a dance lesson.'

'Gee, thanks,' snorted Lee.

'Hey, Woolly,' hissed Webbo. 'You'd better wear your tutu.'

I wasn't quite sure what a tutu was, and I was happy not to know.

'Any questions?' asked Mr Clarke, putting the top on his pen and shuffling the untidy pile of books on his desk. I stared at them, hoping I'd managed to rub out the worst of Webbo's handiwork, then jumped as I heard his voice. It seemed as if I only had to think of him to conjure him up like a wicked genie out of a bottle.

'Yes,' announced Webbo. 'Why do the boys have to do it? It's girls' stuff.'

'Cissy,' added Carl.

'Does anybody else agree with John?' asked Mr Clarke. It sounded funny hearing Webbo's real name. Only the teachers ever used it.

A few hands darted up, all boys. After a persuasive glare from Webbo, another half-dozen raised their hands.

'And who disagrees?'

About half the girls raised their hands.

'Mm,' said Mr Clarke. 'Well, it's an interesting division of opinion. Why's it cissy, boys?'

Without asking for anyone else's opinion, Webbo answered on behalf of the boys. 'Oh, you know, all that prancing round with your arms in the air. I mean, it's stupid.'

'Why is it?' asked Lianne. 'Male ballet dancers have to be really strong and athletic.'

'Oh yeah,' sneered Webbo.

'Says who?' added Vinny.

'Lianne's right, you know,' said Mr Clarke. 'Dance is all about strength, balance, controlling your own body. It's very demanding.'

'It's stupid,' interrupted Carl.

'So do we get out of it?' asked Webbo. 'Girls for dance, boys for football.'

Mr Clarke gave him a cool stare. 'I'm afraid not. Like it or not, John, there's a dance lesson this Monday and everybody's doing it. Everybody.'

Realizing the subject was closed, everybody headed for their lunch boxes.

'Have you got a minute, Davy?' asked Mr Clarke, as I rose, pushing my chair back.

I stopped, letting the class swarm out around me.

'Pop over here a sec,' he said, taking my silence as assent. He stared levelly at me through his glasses. There was something in his expression that told me he had a good idea of what was going on. 'Any problems, Davy?' he began.

'What do you mean, Mr Clarke?' I asked.

'Is somebody giving you a hard time?'

I shrugged.

'You don't seem very happy,' he continued. 'You're not taking much care in your work, either. I've noticed a change over the last couple of weeks. Would you like to tell me about it?'

I spied Webbo peering through the classroom window. I lowered my eyes.

'Davy?'

'Yes, Mr Clarke?'

'I asked you if you'd like to tell me about it? I want to help.'

It wasn't that I didn't want to reply; I just daren't.

'I can't do anything unless you tell me what's wrong, you know,' he added.

'There's nothing wrong,' I mumbled, glancing furtively at Webbo and his mates as they jabbed their fingers at me behind Mr Clarke's back.

'Sure?' he asked in a voice that showed he was far from convinced.

I nodded.

'OK, off you go,' he said.

I stepped gratefully away from his desk and picked up my packed lunch.

'What did Clarkey want?' demanded Webbo, as I emerged from the classroom.

'He asked me if anything was wrong,' I explained.

'What did you say?'

'I said no.'

'You took a long time to say no,' said Vinny.

'He kept asking me,' I replied. 'I didn't say anything, honest.'

'Well, keep your mouth shut or you'll really get it,' warned Webbo.

With that, the three of them sauntered off. I gave a sigh of relief, thank goodness they didn't feel like baiting me any more. I turned my face into the fresh breeze and closed my eyes.

'Far side, Carl,' came Webbo's voice. 'Cross it, cross it!'

I opened my eyes to see Carl striking a football low across the goalmouth painted on the wall. Webbo was on hand to volley it hard past Sean Phelan.

'Goal!' bellowed Webbo, slapping palms with the rest of his team.

He was genuinely popular. He didn't have to bully anyone else. They really liked him. So why me? Why did he have it in for me? I can't say I wanted to be his mate or anything like that, but if he would just say something nice to me I'd gladly forget all the insults. I turned away from the game and sat on the step near the dustbins. The caretaker wandered by and tossed some cardboard boxes in. He gave me a wink as he walked past. Alone again, I hugged the lunch box to my stomach and stared ahead of me, not focussing on anything in particular. Suddenly Vinny came crashing into me, charging after a loose ball. He staggered back, winded, as Terry Morgan pounced on the ball and scampered off towards the goal.

'You made me lose that,' he spat savagely.

'I never!' I countered. 'You fell over my legs.'

'Then keep them in,' ordered Vinny, lashing out at my shins.

'What's up, Vin,' asked Carl. 'Woolly the Wimp giving you trouble?'

'Tripped me up, didn't he?' complained Vinny. I think he really did believe it was my fault.

'You've got to watch yourself,' said Webbo, joining his mates. 'You can't keep getting in our way. We might just get annoyed.'

I looked up at the trio.

'Watch it,' advised Vinny. 'Just watch it, that's all.'

I didn't get a chance to reply, even if I'd wanted to. One of the dinner ladies gave a loud blast on her whistle. The Infants were finished. It was our turn to go in for dinners. I joined the press of bodies around the doorway. I saw Lianne Whalley looking across at me.

'Are you going tonight, Davy?' she asked.

'I've got to,' I replied morosely. 'Anna's going so Mum wants me to come as well.'

'It'll be a laugh,' said Lianne. 'It's not the teachers doing it, you know. It's a proper disco.'

That's what I was afraid of, is what I thought.

'Oh,' is what I said.

Lianne obviously found me a bit boring. She drifted off towards the other girls. I shrugged my shoulders. It was becoming a habit. Left on my own again. I put my foot on the step and reached for the door jamb.

'Stop shoving!' shouted Mrs Binns, the head dinner-lady.

I tried to step back. That's when it happened. The body in front of me suddenly moved away. With a start I realized it was Carl. Why hadn't I noticed him before? Carl's movement was followed by a sharp kick on the ankle and a shove from behind. There was no saving me.

With a surprised grunt, I tumbled forward and fell into the corridor; my lunch box went spinning from my hand.

'There,' announced Mrs Binns angrily. 'That's what happens when you push. Come on, get back you lot.'

As the crowd thinned around me, I rose unsteadily to my feet. I hadn't felt any pain when I fell, but I was definitely shaky and my right knee hurt. I didn't need to look around to work out who'd tripped me. I could already hear Webbo's voice.

'We told you to watch your feet,' he taunted. 'You won't be any good in Clarkey's dance lesson.'

'Clumsy, aren't they, these Woollybacks?' added Vinny.

The back of my neck was hot and itchy. I felt more embarrassed than angry.

'Where's your lunch box, son?' asked Mrs Binns.

I found it by the staffroom door. The red plastic catch was cracked. It had been stamped on. The carton of orange had burst and was spilling on to the tiled floor. It looked as if my sandwiches had been kicked around like a football. The chocolate biscuits had gone.

'It looks like you'll be needing a school dinner, doesn't it?' asked Mrs Binns. 'You can't eat these now.'

I stared dumbly at the mess. In my mind's eye, I could just see my three tormentors trampling my lunch box.

'Come on,' urged Mrs Binns. 'I'll order you a dinner.'

As I joined the back of the line for school dinners, I heard Webbo, 'I don't half like the taste of these chockie biscuits, Woolly,' he said. 'Tell your Mum to put them in again.'

Vinny and Carl roared with appreciative laughter. I stared straight ahead.

'Yes?' asked the dinner lady.

I inspected the choice; luke-warm cheese pie, or pastry bobbing in watery mince.

'Cheese pie, please,' I said.

I searched the dining room for a spare chair. I eventually found one, and joined the Year Five girls, setting off a wave of giggles. Sitting at that table I felt as if a spotlight was trained on me, and a loud-speaker was announcing to the whole school – *Here sits Woolly the Wimp*.

On his way past, Webbo leaned forward. 'Just the place for you,' he observed. 'You wimp.'

CHAPTER SIX

Sisters are Good for Something

'Oh, Davy,' was how Mum greeted me after school. 'What a long face!'

I didn't say a word; I just stared into space.

'Don't I even get a hello?' she asked.

'Hello,' I mumbled.

Anna was dancing up and down impatiently. 'Mu-um,' she droned. 'We've got to get home quick. It's the disco tonight.'

'You'll have to wait a minute longer,' said Mum. 'It looks like your big brother has forgotten something.'

'What's that?' I asked.

'Your lunch box,' she explained. 'You've left it in the classroom.'

'I haven't.'

'Where is it, then?'

'Broken.'

'I beg your pardon?'

'I dropped it, and it broke.'

'Oh, Davy,' wailed Mum. 'I only bought it last week. What happened?'

'I just dropped it, that's all. I had to have a school dinner instead.'

'But how?' Mum gave me one of those looks that made me feel I'd let her down.

'I dropped it,' I said impatiently. 'I dropped it, OK? It was an accident.'

It was Mum's turn to stare at me. Somehow she knew there was more to this than I was letting on. The strange thing is that I didn't even think of explaining about Webbo and his mates. In spite of everything I felt that they were right. Yes, Woolly the Wimp, that was me.

'Well,' said Mum, 'You'd better not break the next one. If this becomes a habit you'll be straight back on school dinners.'

I watched Webbo and Carl play-fighting across the yard. They were laughing and enjoying one another's company. They were having fun. There really must be something wrong with me.

'Did you hear what I said, Davy?' she asked.

'Yes, Mum, I heard.'

'You're going to have to pull your socks up, young man.'

My heart sank. When Mum started calling me *young man*, it meant I was going to get my ear bent.

'*Are* you listening?'

'Yes, Mum.'

She glanced at her watch. 'Oh, I can't waste any more time with you now. I've got to be home for four o'clock. Gran's coming down for a few days.'

Thank goodness for grandmothers, I thought.

By now Anna was tugging at Mum's arm for all she was worth. 'Come on, Mum,' she squealed. 'I've got to get ready.'

'You've got two hours yet,' said Mum. 'Just calm down.'

Asking our Anna to calm down was like asking a lion to become a vegetarian. Still, if Mum wanted to waste her breath, that was up to her. Giving me a stony stare, she turned on her heel and set off down the school path. 'We'll talk about all this later, Davy.'

All this! She knew something was bothering me, all right. We were too alike for it to be otherwise. I was following Mum and Anna on to the main road when I heard Webbo and Carl's parting shot.

'See you tonight, Woolly,' called Carl. 'They do requests, you know.'

Wait for it, I told myself, Webbo's bound to have the punchline.

He did. 'They might have your song, Woolly.'

I wasn't going to take the bait. I just hoped Mum didn't realize that they were taking a rise out of me. Without looking back, I turned left on to Bride Lane. As I kept pace with Mum and Anna I heard Webbo and Carl singing at the top of their voices:

Where 'as 'ta been since I saw thee
On Ilkley Moor ba' tat . . .

'Do you know those two, Davy?' asked Mum.

'What?'

'Those two boys. They were talking to you, weren't they?'

'I don't know.'

'Well, I do,' she stated firmly.

Anna was looking from Mum to me and back again, mystified by the exchange.

'Is that what all this moodiness is about?' continued Mum. 'A couple of idiots with nothing better to do than name-calling?'

Yes, is what I thought.

'Just leave it, will you?' is what I said.

'Oh no, Davy,' she snapped, catching me by the sleeve and spinning me round to face her. 'That's just what I won't do. I want to know what's going on, *exactly* what's going on.'

Mum must have caught sight of Anna's startled little face about the same time I did.

'I'll talk to you later,' she said. 'Don't think I've finished with you yet, Davy lad. No, not by a long chalk.'

Anna gave us a last puzzled look before turning to her pet subject.

'Can I wear my new dress?' she asked. 'I won't get it dirty.'

'Sorry, my love?' asked Mum, not really concentrating on Anna.

'My dress,' repeated Anna. 'The purple one. Can I wear it tonight?'

'Yes,' said Mum, smiling at last. 'That's what I got it for.'

Anna's face lit up with pleasure.

'You go and play upstairs,' Mum told Anna, as she opened the front door. 'Your brother and I have got things to discuss.'

'Oh, Mum,' I said unhappily. 'I told you it was nothing.'

'And I know it isn't. Come on, Anna, upstairs with you. Now.'

'Can I get my dress out?' asked Anna.

'Yes. But don't get it dirty.'

I watched Anna thundering upstairs, then turned to face the music.

'Right,' Mum began. 'Spill the beans.'

The beans stayed in the can. Before I could say a word, the doorbell rang. Gran, God bless her!

'Have you got a fiver, love?' she asked, as Mum opened the door. 'The taxi driver hasn't got any change for this twenty.'

Mum paid the fare and glanced meaningfully at Gran's suitcase. I took the hint and lugged it into the hall. Then, ignoring Mum's You're-not-off-the-hook-yet look, I led the way into the living room.

'Is that Gran?' yelled Anna, bounding downstairs.

'That's right,' said Gran, holding her arms out for a hug.

'I'm going to a disco,' said Anna.

'A disco!' repeated Gran. How did she always manage to sound interested in the most stupid things?

'I'm wearing my new dress,' continued Anna. 'Do you want to see it?'

'Of course I do,' said Gran. 'Lead the way.'

'Oh,' spluttered Anna, her face falling. 'No, we can't go upstairs. I'll bring it down.'

Webbo and his mates had almost made me forget the Something-She-Brought-Back in Anna's room. Mum certainly hadn't forgotten. I knew by the expression on her face as she stared after Anna that she was going to get to the bottom of that, too.

'And how are you, Davy?' asked Gran.

'I'm all right,' I said flatly.

Mum sucked her teeth, making a tut-tutting noise, but she didn't contradict me openly.

'There!' cried Anna, charging back into the living room with the dress.

'Oh, isn't it lovely,' said Gran. 'You'll be a real little princess in it.'

Some princess! Grubby hands, a runny nose and a voice that could curdle milk.

'Oh,' said Gran, remembering something. 'Where's that carrier bag you took off me, Sandra?'

'I put it in the kitchen,' replied Mum.

'Come on, you two,' said Gran. 'I've got a few little pressies.'

As I followed Gran into the kitchen, I noticed Mum slipping into the hallway. I wanted to warn Anna, I couldn't. All I could do was wait for the fireworks to begin.

'You haven't got that one, have you?' asked Gran anxiously.

'No, it's great.' I inspected the computer game. How did she do it? Of all the grans in the whole world, was there another one who never bought a naff present?

'Not too told for Winnie-the-Pooh, are you, Anna!' she asked, presenting The Mouth with a video and honey-coloured teddy bear.

Anna was delighted, for a least ten seconds. Ten seconds was the time between her hugging the teddy and Mum appearing in the kitchen doorway. 'Anna,' she said in her lowest, most menacing growl. 'You can forget the disco. You're staying in tonight.'

Forget the disco! So sisters were good for something, after all.

CHAPTER SEVEN
Chicken!

'Whatever is the matter, Sandra?' asked Gran.

She looked at Anna for a clue, but for once my talkative little sister was quite tongue-tied. She just stared at the floor and tried to shrink into Gran's lap.

'I've got a bone to pick with our Anna,' said Mum breathlessly. 'A chicken bone, to be more precise.'

'I beg your pardon?' said Gran.

'Follow me,' ordered Mum. 'In this case, seeing is believing.'

Gran, Anna and I followed Mum up the stairs like the condemned mounting the scaffold. Quite why Gran looked guilty I wasn't sure, but she always seemed to take our side against our parents.

'There!' announced Mum, flinging open the door.

What hit me first was the smell.

'Good grief!' gasped Gran, holding a handkerchief to her face. 'What is it?'

'It,' said Mum, 'is in the cat litter.'

'Surely the cat doesn't smell this bad,' said Gran.

'He doesn't,' agreed Mum. 'Look.'

We looked. Mum drew back the duvet to reveal a small, black-and-red hen.

'It's a chicken! gasped Gran and I together.

'It is,' huffed Mum. 'And unlike Flapjack, it doesn't know how to use a litter tray. The mess is everywhere. Anna, how could you? I don't know how I'll ever get rid of the smell.'

'But how did you stand the stink all night?' I asked.

'And where did you get it?' asked Gran.

Mum's face drained of blood; she clearly hadn't got round to thinking about that. There was a long pause, as if time was ticking by in slow motion. At last Mum's eyes widened. 'Oh Anna, you didn't!'

'Didn't what?' asked Gran, thoroughly confused by the whole thing.

'You couldn't,' said Mum.

'Couldn't what?' asked Gran.

'Oh, not on the . . .' Mum's voice faltered. 'You wouldn't.'

That's when Gran's patience finally snapped. 'Sandra!' she roared. 'Where did she get it?'

'The farm,' said Mum. 'You brought it back from the farm, didn't you, Anna?'

Anna nodded.

'In your bag. That's why you wouldn't let me carry it, wasn't it?'

Anna nodded again.

'And hid it in your room. That's why . . .' Mum finally stopped stating the obvious. Anna was now nodding before she'd even been asked. 'Oh, Anna,' Mum groaned again.

'Look, Sandra,' Gran began, before she was cut off in mid-sentence.

'Not this time,' Mum interrupted. 'I'm not letting her off this time. Anna has to learn her lesson. The disco is off. Off, I say.'

Oh joy! I felt like hugging my little tyke of a sister, but

in the circumstances I didn't think it would have gone down too well with anyone.

'Stay put, young lady,' ordered Mum. 'I'm going to try to clean your room before I go to work, and you're going to help me.'

Our Colin had the bad luck to open the front door just as Hurricane Sandra passed by.

'What's for tea?' he grunted.

Mum said nothing. What came out was more of an exasperated scream.

Colin stood in the hall staring after her. 'What's up with Mum?' he asked.

'Anna,' I said.

'What?'

'Anna's what's up with Mum,' I repeated.

'Am I missing something here?' he asked, looking even more dopey than usual.

'Anna stole a chicken,' I explained.

'Oh yeah,' smirked Colin. 'And I'm riding a unicycle.'

'I did!' cried Anna. 'I took a chicken. It's a batman.'

'Don't you mean Robin?' quipped Colin, still unsure whether to take any of this seriously.

'I've got a chicken,' insisted Anna. 'And it is a batman, Mrs Collins said so.'

'Oh, Anna,' I chuckled, realizing what she meant. 'Not a batman, a bantam.'

Colin plodded into the kitchen in search of food, muttering, 'Chicken, I ask you.' He was on his way back into the living room when Mum stamped back downstairs holding the Something-Anna-Brought-Back. It was only a little Something, but that was no consolation to Mum. She was furious.

'It's a chicken!' gasped Colin, letting the paste butty fall from his mouth.

'We did tell you,' I said, in my most superior voice.

'And it's called Batman?' asked Colin.

'I don't care if he's called Superman,' said Mum. 'He goes back.'

'But Mum!' cried Anna.

'But nothing,' said Mum firmly. 'Don't you understand? You stole this chicken.'

'Only a little bit,' said Anna.

'Anna,' sighed Mum. 'You can't steal something *a little bit*. Stealing is stealing, and it's wrong.'

'But he was lonely,' said Anna.

'No wonder,' said Colin, wrinkling his nose. 'This is one smelly little chicken.'

'I thought you said there were hundreds of chickens,' I interrupted.

'Yeah,' added Colin, 'All going *Batman, dinner dinner dinner dinner*.'

Colin laughed. Nobody else did.

'No ifs, no buts,' said Mum. 'On Monday morning we're going in early to see Mrs Collins. Then back he goes.'

'Aw, poor Batman,' giggled Colin.

Anna gazed imploringly at Gran, but Gran just shrugged her shoulders. 'Mum's right this time, love,' she said, earning a disgusted glare from Mum for the *this* time. 'He isn't ours. He'll have to go back.'

Now, if Colin's timing was bad, Dad's was even worse. In the middle of all this, in he swept with Billy King from work. They were carrying a huge rabbit hutch.

'Ta ra!' announced Dad, beaming all over his silly face. 'I'm buying the rabbit next week.'

Colin laughed, I spluttered, Gran raised her eyes to the ceiling and Anna winced. Mum blew her top. 'This,' she fumed, 'is a madhouse.'

With that, she pulled on her coat and made for the door. 'I'm going to work,' she shouted.

'What's for tea?' asked Dad.

'Chicken!' cried Mum.

'I like chicken,' said Dad, innocent of all the goings-on. 'Have you got time to stop for your tea, Bill?'

'I'll have to phone home,' said Billy.

'OK. You phone home, and our Col will get the chicken.' Dad sat down at the table. I gave Colin a bewildered stare.

'Well,' said Colin. 'Get the plates.'

I did as I was told while Anna and Gran looked on, lost for words.

'Right,' said Dad, as Billy sat down. 'Where's this chicken?'

Colin plucked Batman from behind Anna's back and deposited him on Dad's plate. 'There!'

Batman gave Dad a cold, indifferent stare and scratched at the plate.

'Colin,' murmured Dad.

'Yes, Dad?'

'It's a chicken.'

'You can't pull the wool over your eyes,' Colin said with a mischievous smile.

'Ray,' said Billy, rising from the table. 'I think I'll go home for tea after all.'

CHAPTER EIGHT
Just Another Saturday Afternoon

'Well,' demanded Dad. 'Are you coming or not?'

'I don't know.' I did know, but I couldn't bring myself to tell Dad that his special treat was about as exciting as week-old apple crumble.

'Don't know!' snorted Dad. 'Don't know! Look, Davy, I'm talking about Liverpool Football Club. You know, Anfield, You'll Never Walk Alone, The Kop . . .'

'Come on, Davy,' urged Colin. 'You'll enjoy it.'

Dad gave me a despairing look. 'Leave him, Col. He'd rather hang around the house.'

I didn't contradict him. The match was his idea of a big treat and I hated disappointing him, but I just wasn't interested. Dad was a sports fiend. It had been his way of keeping busy when he was made redundant. Circuit training every Wednesday, swimming on a Sunday and, in-between, a captive audience for every minute of televised sport. The only book he was interested in was the one in the referee's breast pocket. Fortunately, Dad soon forgot about me and got his claws into Mum.

'Fancy a spin when I get back from the match, Sandra?'

'No way,' said Mum, unloading the washing machine. 'You'll never learn if you don't try.'

'I am learning. I've got a lesson at three o'clock.'

'Lesson!' exclaimed Dad. 'But I can teach you. Lessons cost a fortune.'

'I'm taking lessons,' said Mum stubbornly. 'I'm not having you yelling down my ear all the time.'

'Me? Me, yell?'

'That's right, Ray,' said Mum, filling the drier. 'And you've yelled your last at this driver.'

Dad shook his head and stamped into the garden.

'What's up with Ray?' asked Gran, as she appeared with Anna in tow.

'He doesn't like me having lessons,' explained Mum. 'He wants to teach me himself.'

'I wouldn't let our Ray teach you,' said Gran. 'That son of mine is like a bear with a sore head when it comes to his precious car.'

'Don't I know it,' murmured Mum wryly.

Tired of the family arguments, I wandered upstairs. Once I was in the safety of my room, I began to relax. I hated the interrogation downstairs. I ask you, even my dad thought I was a wimp.

'Are you all right, Davy?' asked Colin, sticking his head round the door. 'Mum seems to think there's something wrong?'

'Oh no, what's she been saying now?'

'Not much,' said Colin. 'She thought you might need cheering up.'

'I'm fine, honest.'

'Oh, have it your own way,' he sighed, withdrawing his head.

'Colin,' I called. 'Hang on.'

'What's up?'

'I'm worried about you.'

'Me!' said Colin. 'You're worried about me?'

'Yes,' I replied. 'I know it sounds daft, but you're playing with fire. I know who you're hanging round with.'

'Oh, give over,' he said. 'You sound just like Mum. I can take care of myself.'

'Oh, sure you can, hard man,' I scoffed. 'I tell you straight, Col, if it comes to a fight with a car, you're going to lose.'

'What are you talking about?' He tried to sound unconcerned, but he was rattled. He was blinking rapidly.

'You know exactly what I'm talking about,' I continued. 'That stupid game Ricky Scholes has got you playing.'

'Have you been spying on me?' He was really fidgety now. He liked to put on the streetwise act, but it didn't suit him.

'Yes.' Well, why deny it?

'You won't tell Mum and Dad, will you?'

'That's up to you.'

'Meaning?' Colin was annoyed, but more than a bit scared.

'Meaning you've got to stop that stupid game. You'll get yourself killed.'

'But they're my mates,' he whined.

'With mates like that, who needs enemies?' I answered.

Colin wasn't to be outdone. 'With brothers like you, who needs parents?' he concluded.

'Are you going to stop it?' I asked. 'I don't want a dead brother.' Of course I didn't. We'd always been really close.

'I don't plan to end up dead,' said Colin. 'It's just a lark.'

'Some lark!' I bawled, losing my temper.

'Hey,' came Dad's voice. 'What's all the yelling about?'

Colin turned pleading eyes on me. He looked just like Anna. Why did I end up protecting everybody's secrets?

'He won't keep out of my room,' I said. 'I just want a bit of peace.'

Colin relaxed.

'Well, you don't need to shout the house down,' grumbled Dad. 'I don't know what's up with you just lately. You used to be such a great kid. You're becoming a real pain in the neck, do you know that?'

I did.

'Come on, Colin,' he continued. 'Let's get off to the match.'

I listened to their footsteps on the stairs and the door slamming. My heart ached. There had been a time when the family was everything to me, but it seemed to be falling apart. Well, Davy lad, I thought, you handled that well.

'Davy,' shouted Mum suddenly from the hallway, 'Is it up there?'

'What?'

'The chicken, is it upstairs?'

'I don't know.'

'Well, look for him,' scolded Mum. 'Anna's in floods of tears down here.'

So there was I a few minutes later searching the bedrooms, calling out in my best David Attenborough voice: 'Here, Batman!'

'Any luck?' called Mum.

'Give me a chance,' I answered.

I looked under the beds, in the beds, behind the chairs, in the toy boxes, cupboards, and wardrobes. I even looked down the toilet! No Batman.

'Well?'

'Not up here, Mum.'

I walked downstairs and entered the living room. Anna was crying her eyes out, while Gran did her best to comfort her.

'I don't believe it,' growled Mum. 'I just don't believe it. First my daughter kidnaps the thing, then she loses it. What do I tell Mrs Collins?'

'Don't tell her anything,' I advised. 'She probably doesn't even know anybody took the chicken.'

'Davy,' said Mum, appalled. 'That would be dishonest.'

'Only a little bit,' I said.

'Are you trying to wind me up?' asked Mum. 'That's what Anna said.'

'Oh,' I stammered. 'I thought I'd heard it somewhere.'

'I give up,' said Mum. 'I really do give up.'

That's when I heard it. It was like one of those silly jokes that goes round school every now and then; what goes *scrape tap scrape tap*?

'Now what?' sighed Mum.

What goes *scrape tap scrape tap*?

I followed the sound across the living room and into the kitchen. 'It's coming from in here,' I announced, looking round.

Well, what goes *scrape tap scrape tap*? A fridge with a wooden leg, a rhinoceros in a microwave? No, I'll tell you what goes *scrape tap scrape tap*: a chicken in a washing machine.

'Look who's here,' I called, reaching in for Batman.

'You've found him!' squealed Anna. 'Hiya Batman.'

'But who shut the poor thing in there?' asked Gran.

'I think he got in by himself,' I replied. 'Somebody must have shut the door on him.'

'It's a good job nobody turned the machine on, isn't it?' chuckled Gran.

I tried to imagine Batman on fast spin. It didn't bear thinking about. I looked from Mum to Gran, and from Gran to Anna. Ho hum, just another barmy Saturday afternoon.

CHAPTER NINE
Coming Clean

I pulled on the reverse for the umpteenth time that Sunday morning.

'Anna!' I yelled. 'If you do that again, I'll go mad.'

'You're mad already,' she yelled back. If I was, it must run in the family. My brother was hanging round with kids who'd make Al Capone look cuddly, my sister was a hen-napper, and I felt as if I was in training to be a World Champion doormat for every bully to wipe his feet on.

'Don't jump over his car, Anna,' said Mum softly. 'It cost a lot of money.'

One hundred pounds, to be precise. I'd always wanted a really good remote control. Even Webbo had to admit it was impressive, the time I took it into school.

'I won't hurt it,' said Anna. 'I'm only playing.'

'Here's an axe,' I suggested. 'Go and play on the M6.'

'Davy!' cried Mum. 'Where did you learn to talk like that? Say sorry to your sister.'

'Sorry.' I wasn't. Anna, like the rest of the world, was getting on my nerves. It was eleven o'clock on Sunday morning and I was already dreading school. That grey cloud was forming over my head. I hit the forward button and sent the car bouncing over the gravel path. Webbo had ruined school for me, now he was chipping away at weekends. It was Saturday afternoon before I forgot about him and by Sunday dinner I was already anticipating the first taunts of a new week.

Anna's voice interrupted my thoughts. 'Isn't Davy coming?'

'No,' said Gran. 'He's got to have a talk with your mum.'

I stared at Mum.

'Don't argue,' she warned. 'You've got things to tell me.'

With a sinking heart I watched Gran and Anna set off hand-in-hand towards the lake. Anna had taken the heat off me since Mum discovered Batman in her room. Now that was over, and there was no way I could stand up to Mum when she had me cornered like this.

'Put the car away,' said Mum. She was using her patient-but-firm voice, which always worried me more than the angry-but-hairless one she usually used when one of us had done something wrong.

I unzipped my holdall and reluctantly deposited the car and handset. 'You've got it wrong, Mum,' I protested feebly.

'Oh no, Davy. You've got it wrong. If you think I'm prepared to watch you getting unhappier every day, then you don't know me very well. You're my son and I can tell when something's wrong.'

I shouldered the bag, and dug my hands deep in my trouser pockets.

'OK, Davy, now give.'

'Please, Mum,' I begged. 'Leave it. You'll only make it worse.'

'That's up to me,' said Mum, unmoved. 'I'm waiting.'

I gave a big sigh. 'It's those lads,' I began. 'The two you saw and another boy.'

'Yes.'

'They've been pushing me around.'

Mum raised her eyebrows. 'Keep talking.'

'Oh, you know what it's like,' I said. 'Sometimes they tease me, call me names. Other times they get really angry and start doing things.'

'What sort of things?'

'They broke my lunch box and took my biscuit.' It sounded stupid when I said it like that, but it still bothered me.

'Go on,' said Mum, still composed.

'They tripped me up; that's how it happened. They just tripped me up and kicked my dinner all round the floor.' I could feel my cheeks redden. I was talking fast, and with a flush of anger that surprised myself. 'Webbo—'

'Who's he?'

'John Webster,' I explained. 'Webbo even ate my biscuit right in front of my eyes. They wrote on my book too.'

'What does Mr Clarke say about all this?' asked Mum hotly. She was angry *for* me, not with me.

'I haven't told him,' I admitted.

'What?'

'Oh, how could I, Mum? There's three of them, and—'

'And what?'

I kicked a stone and stared across the park. 'Well, it's me, isn't it?'

'I beg your pardon?' Mum looked confused.

'It's my fault,' I went on uncertainly. 'I mean, they don't pick on anybody else, just me.'

'You don't believe that, do you?'

'I don't know.' I couldn't look Mum in the eye.

'Davy, do you really think it's your fault?'

I nodded glumly.

'Oh, you silly boy. You silly, silly lad. Of course it isn't your fault. They've got the problem, not you.'

I heard her, but I wasn't convinced.

'I'll have a word with Mr Clarke tomorrow,' she continued.

A wave of panic swept through me. 'Oh, Mum, you can't!'

'You don't want this to carry on, do you?' she demanded.

'But you'll make it worse,' I cried. 'They'll batter me. All the kids hate snitching. This girl in Year Five told on somebody and she got called a grass. Her parents had to take her to another school, Craig told me.'

'Davy,' said Mum, 'I really do have to tell Mr Clarke. It won't go away. If we let them get away with it now, they'll keep on doing it. You'll be at the same High School as these boys, you know.'

I stared at her. How could she do this to me? It was all right for her, she didn't have to face them in the playground. I did, and I was going to be alone. Even Craig wandered off when Webbo and his pals appeared. I didn't blame him, they didn't mind him when he wasn't with me.

'I think we'd better tell your dad, don't you?'

I pulled a face. Oh, he was really going to be sympathetic, wasn't he?

'Something wrong?' Mum asked, noticing my expression.

'No, nothing wrong,' I replied.

'Spit it out, Davy.'

'Dad thinks the same way as them,' I remarked.

'I don't think that's fair,' she protested.

'He thinks I'm a wimp, doesn't he?' I shrieked bitterly. 'That's what they call me, Woolly the Wimp.'

'Your dad's never said anything like that, has he?' asked Mum quietly, as if half-convinced that I was right.

'Not in so many words,' I answered. 'But that's

54

what he thinks. Like yesterday over that football match. Colin's the one he likes.'

'He loves the bones of all three of you,' said Mum. She sounded hurt at what I'd said. 'Your dad would never love any of you more than the others. How can you think that way?'

I turned away. 'Here come Gran and Anna,' I said. I noticed Gran and Mum exchange glances. Gran was already in on my troubles.

Dad was back from the Sports Centre by the time we got home. 'Hi,' he called cheerily. When Anna was the only one to return his greeting, he frowned. 'Something wrong?'

'Come on, Anna,' said Gran. 'Let's go into the garden with Batman.'

'Well?' asked Dad. 'Is somebody going to tell me what's going on?'

'Some boys at school are bullying our Davy,' explained Mum.

'Oh,' sighed Dad in relief. 'Is that all?'

'All!' cried Mum. 'Didn't you hear me, Ray? Three young thugs are making his life a misery.'

'It won't last long,' said Dad. 'I got bullied for a while when I was a kid. It'll blow over, you'll see.'

'Is that all you've got to say?' asked Mum.

'What do you expect? It's lad-like, part of growing up.' Dad reached for the newspaper.

Mum stared at him, dumbfounded. 'Don't tell me you think it's all right?'

'Come on, Davy,' said Dad, reluctantly sliding his paper back into the rack. 'Tell me what they've done.'

'They broke my lunch box,' I replied. 'And they push me around and call me names . . .'

'What names?'

I looked at Mum. 'Tell him,' she ordered.

'They call me Woolly the Wimp.'

Dad burst out laughing. 'Woolly the Wimp?'

'Ray!' cried Mum. 'What do you think you're laughing at?'

'Sorry,' said Dad. 'I didn't mean to; it's just . . .'

I hated him for laughing. He *did* think like them. I knew he did.

'Just what?' asked Mum. She was furious.

'Oh, don't get upset, love,' protested Dad. 'I only meant it sounded funny.'

'It isn't funny to our Davy,' said Mum sharply.

'I think you're going over the top about this,' said Dad. 'You know the lad's a bit thin-skinned. He's got to learn to mix, that's all.'

'You're worse than those bullies,' Mum cried suddenly.

'Sandra!' said Dad, standing up. 'Don't say that. I'd do anything for my kids. How can you compare me to a gang of bullies?'

'You're just like them,' Mum insisted. 'You're his dad and you don't care when a gang of kids are terrorizing the poor lad.'

'Don't start getting angry,' said Dad, 'Nobody will take you seriously if you start talking like that.'

'So what do you propose to do about it?' asked Mum.

'I don't suppose there's much we can do,' Dad replied.

'We could see his teacher.'

'Is that what you want, Davy?' asked Dad. I think he had begun to realize how upset I was. 'Well, is it?'

I stared at the carpet. I had this feeling that they weren't even arguing about me any more. They were just arguing for the sake of it.

'Well?' he continued. 'Do you want me and your mum to see Mr Clarke?'

'No, Dad.'

56

'There you are,' he said, sounding relieved. 'If he doesn't want us to go in, it can't be that serious.'

Mum glared at me as if I'd let her down, but I hadn't. I just didn't want everybody knowing I'd run to my parents like a coward. I'd never live it down.

'Davy!' cried Mum. 'Tell him. Tell your dad how you really feel?'

I shook my head. 'I'm all right.'

The trouble is, I wasn't.

CHAPTER TEN
Support

'I'm going to feel a right prat,' grumbled Craig.

'You are a right prat,' giggled Hanif, as he shoved past to get his PE kit.

Craig pulled a face. 'I suppose I asked for that,' he said with a grin. 'Are you OK, Davy?'

'Me?' I asked. 'Yes, I'm fine.'

I wasn't really listening; I'd been stealing glances at Webbo and his mates for the last five minutes. They'd been a bit too quiet for my liking. I just couldn't win. If they were tormenting me I was miserable, and if they weren't, I was just as anxious wondering what they were planning!

'Right,' said Clarkey, clapping his hands for attention. 'This is the lady I told you about from the college. Her name is Mrs Vanzetti.' His voice faltered; he wasn't sure of the pronunciation. Reassured by a smile from the newcomer who was standing beside him, he continued. 'Mrs Vanzetti is a dance tutor, and I've invited her to take you for a dance lesson. Over to you then, Mrs Vanzetti.'

'She doesn't look German,' said Craig.

'That's not a German name,' hissed Lianne, loud enough to be heard across the classroom.

'Quite right,' Mrs Vanzetti interrupted with a smile. 'My husband is Italian.'

The strong Scottish accent told us that she wasn't.

Everybody was giggling and nudging one another at Lianne's over-loud whisper, so Clarkey raised his voice.

'Calm down, please. I'd like you to listen.'

I don't think Mrs Vanzetti appreciated the assistance. She seemed the sort of person who liked to do things her own way. Clarkey got the message and left her to it.

'Now,' she said quietly, 'I'm sure your teacher got some funny looks when he told you about today.'

'You can say that again,' sniggered Carl.

'I'm sure some of you – especially the boys – will feel a bit self-conscious,' Mrs Vanzetti continued. 'Well, let me assure you that you shouldn't.'

She carried on for a few moments about how important dance was for fitness and how she had helped train a couple of professional footballers using dance techniques. The mind boggled – Gazza in ballet shoes!

'Now,' said Mrs Vanzetti, 'If you'd like to walk into the hall and find a space.'

Webbo started jigging about, and soon half the class were clowning it up as they walked down the corridor. Before Clarkey could say a word, Mrs Vanzetti singled out Webbo. 'Do you need the toilet?' she asked.

'No,' said Webbo, clearly wondering what she meant.

'Then do stop that wriggling,' she advised. Tony Gordon snorted with laughter, but stopped abruptly the moment Webbo turned round. His face was bright red. I was warming to Mrs Vanzetti after the way she dealt with him. She was tall, willowy and very dark. 'Face me, please,' she said, pausing while Clarkey noisily drew up a chair to watch. 'Good. Now, we are going to look at how we balance. Could you raise your right foot, please?'

I raised my right foot. She'd won me over for one and I had almost forgotten that I was supposed to be embarrassed.

'Now hold that position,' said Mrs Vanzetti. 'Good,

now can you feel the foot on which you're standing adjusting to keep you up?'

To my amazement, I could. Glancing around to make sure nobody was watching I tried again. Yes, I could actually do it.

'Now lower your foot and—' She was interrupted by a loud thud. Webbo had stamped his flat foot on the floor with all the grace of a baby hippopotamus.

'Oh,' sighed Mrs Vanzetti gently, 'Are you wearing those awful training shoes. The soles are too rigid for dance. Bare feet, please.'

Webbo glared at her. I waited to see how she was going to sort this one out, but she didn't need to. Instead, Clarkey leaned across. 'Off!' he insisted.

'That's better,' said Mrs Vanzetti, giving Clarkey the sort of look that some people give over-full dustbins. 'Now, raise the other foot. Slow-ly. Good. And hold it.'

I noticed Lianne smiling, and smiled back. I heard a derisive snort and glimpsed Vinny and Carl nudging each other.

'Look at that big girl,' cackled Vinny. He didn't mean Lianne.

'He would like this,' commented Webbo. 'He'll be playing with dolls next.'

Make a note, I told myself, smiling at girls is not a good move.

'That's very good,' said Mrs Vanzetti, scanning the class. 'Now, can we try something different? Instead of copying me, raise your foot in a different direction and hold it. That's it, choose a position of your own, and see if you can remain steady.'

As we stretched out our legs and balanced, she walked among us, giving encouragement. 'Good . . . Yes, a little higher . . . Balance remember, don't overdo it and make yourself fall.'

She was standing by Cathy and Brian. 'Fine, now rest. Let's watch you two. What are your names?'

Cathy answered quickly enough but Brian nearly choked on his name. He looked like he wanted the floor to swallow him up. The look on his face provoked loud guffaws.

'Right,' said Mrs Vanzetti, ignoring the mirth. 'Can you all watch Cathy and Brian.' More laughter.

'And rest,' she said. 'Now, who else wants to try? Who'd like to volunteer?

Lianne's hand was up straight away. She loved the attention.

'Good,' said Mrs Vanzetti. 'What's your name? OK, who wants to be Lianne's partner?'

She scanned the room several times before her eyes finally alighted on me: 'What about you? What's your name?'

I heard a hissed 'Woolly the Wimp' behind me.

'Davy,' I croaked inaudibly.

'Daley?' asked Mrs Vanzetti.

'Davy,' I corrected, shouting over the peals of laughter.

'Right,' she said, struggling on. 'Can you all watch Lianne and David?'

More laughter.

I took my position, staring straight ahead to avoid the eyes of the rest of the class.

'And rest,' said Mrs Vanzetti.

'Now, if you wouldn't mind, I'd like to demonstrate one more thing, then your classmates can join in. OK?'

Lianne nodded. I just stood there wishing I could beam up somewhere. I was going to suffer for this.

'David,' Mrs Vanzetti continued. 'I want you to support Lianne in her movement.'

Oh God.

'This will allow Lianne to stretch without falling.'

Oh God, oh God.

'Now don't be afraid of her. She won't bite.'

Oh God, oh God, oh God.

'Now stretch. Good, rely on your partner, Lianne. Davy, hold her. You are supporting her, you know.'

I didn't know what to do with myself. Touching Lianne's leg was making my hand clammy, and I could hear the giggles and whispers. Didn't Mrs Vanzetti know I was squirming with embarrassment? I mean, if this was living, then I just wanted to die.

'That's lovely. Good. And rest.'

Oh, thank goodness. Lianne winked, and I lowered my eyes.

'Now,' said Mrs Vanzetti, 'can we all find a partner?'

We did, but not quite the way she had in mind. I was looking round for Craig when Mrs Vanzetti said pointedly. 'Oh, you're not scared of the girls, are you? What, all you big boys?'

I still hadn't located Craig.

'David doesn't mind working with a young lady, do you, David?'

Yes, I do mind, was what I thought.

'No,' is what I said.

'There,' said Mrs Vanzetti. 'Now, boy girl, boy girl, boy girl.'

I watched her going round the hall pairing up boys and girls. Webbo got stuck with Antonia Plang, which must have cheered him up no end. If people were food, Antonia Plang would be cold rice pudding.

'She's great, isn't she?' whispered Lianne. She meant Mrs Vanzetti, not Antonia Plang.

I made a low noise in my throat, like a dying frog. Lianne took it for agreement, but it was despair. I really was going to suffer for this.

'Support your partner,' ordered Mrs Vanzetti. Webbo dropped Antonia. On purpose, I think. Craig and Shaima crumpled in a hysterical heap.

'OK, OK,' smiled Mrs Vanzetti. 'Now let's take it further.'

The next stage was to run then take up a balancing position.

By the third run I was beginning to forget my surge of panic. I loved the feeling of control. Lianne was the only other kid who could come to rest as quickly as I could. It was like we'd suddenly learned to fly. Our bodies were new, we were magic.

'One more time,' said Mrs Vanzetti. She had the class eating out of her hand. Even Webbo had stopped clowning.

I ran and rose on to my right foot, bringing my whole body into a stretching, rising position.

'Lovely,' announced Mrs Vanzetti. 'Oh, you are learning quickly.' She turned to confide in Clarkey. 'What a wonderful class you have, Mr Clarke.'

Clarkey smiled a crooked smile. Turning to face us again, Mrs Vanzetti introduced the last part of the lesson. 'Now for our finale,' she announced.

We had to work in pairs again, one partner supporting the other as they ran and came to rest. Lianne raced forward and rose on to her right foot, leaning forward with complete confidence that I would support her. I reached and felt her ribs against my palms.

'Now swop over,' shouted Mrs Vanzetti over the muttering and giggling that followed the movement.

This time I ran forward and rose into my resting position. It was like I was flying again. I just rose and rose, reached and stretched, coming to a halt with Lianne's hands steadying me.

'And rest!' cried Mrs Vanzetti, delighted with the results

of her lesson. I didn't rest. I didn't want to. I just held my position then slowly eased my raised foot to the floor.

'Just look at the Wimp,' sneered Webbo as the class headed for the corridor. 'I might have guessed he'd like prancing about like a big girl.'

My heart sank. Why did I have to forget myself like that? Why did I have to prat about? I'd flown, and now Webbo was going to bring me crashing back to earth. Just when I thought things couldn't get any worse, Mrs Vanzetti drove the final nail in the coffin.

'You and Lianne were very good,' she said. 'You ought to go to a dance class. Why don't you come along to the college? I'm running a course for students. I've got about a dozen volunteers from local schools coming to demonstrate.' She began to write the details on a scrap of notepaper. 'Will you come?' she asked. I could see Webbo and his mates pointing and laughing.

'Oh yes,' said Lianne, taking the note.

'What about you, David?'

I shrugged my shoulders, burning up inside at Webbo's derisive jeers.

'Well,' said Mrs Vanzetti, suddenly aware that she had put me on the spot. 'Think about it, eh?'

Like I said, I was going to suffer for this.

CHAPTER ELEVEN
Chicken or Egg

'Which came first?' chirped a familiar voice behind me.

'What?' I asked, as I turned to face Mum.

'Which came first?' she repeated gaily. 'The chicken or the egg?'

'Are you all right?' I asked.

'Happy's the word, Davy,' she replied. 'You do remember happy?'

What had got into her? She'd been dreading this morning. She had had to take Anna and Batman into Mrs Collins.

'Didn't Mrs Collins mind?' I asked.

'Mind!' exclaimed Mum. 'She thought it was hysterical. She told the whole class and when the kids had stopped laughing, she phoned the farmer, and guess what?'

'What?'

'He's going to show them how to hatch some eggs right there in the classroom.'

'Get away.' I couldn't quite manage to sound excited, but my show of modest interest convinced Mum.

'You should have seen Anna's face. She's thrilled. I thought she'd be really upset giving Batman back, but she's looking forward to all those fluffy, yellow chicks.'

Trust The Mouth to fall on her feet (can mouths fall on their feet?).

'Anyway,' Mum concluded, 'I've got to get down to the supermarket. Is everything all right?' She cast her eyes across the yard at the kids playing.

'Yeah yeah, everything's fine,' I said.

'Where's Craig?' asked Mum.

'He's gone to run a message,' I explained. 'He'll be back in a minute.'

'So you're not on your own, then?'

'No, I told you, everything's fine.' That was the truth, more or less. A few jibes about the Sugarplum Fairy, but nothing serious.

Mum inspected my face for a moment or two, as if she was trying to read my thoughts, then she gave me a peck on the cheek and headed for the school gate.

'See you at a quarter past three, Davy.'

'See you, Mum.'

'See you, Mum,' mimicked Webbo.

'What's for dinner, Daley?' asked Vinny.

'You mean Da-vid, don't you, Vin?' smirked Carl.

'Oh, that's right,' said Vinny. 'Anyway, what's for dinner? Got any of those chockie biscuits?'

'Yes,' added Webbo, 'The ones with the mint filling.'

Drop dead, is what I thought.

'No,' is what I said.

'Want to dance?' asked Carl, taking my arm.

'Notice how we hold our position,' said Webbo, shoving me roughly off balance.

'Leave me alone!' I cried hotly.

'But we thought you liked dancing,' said Vinny, his eyes narrowing.

'That's what he told Just-One-Cornetto,' said Webbo. 'Maybe you only dance with your partner. Hey, Lianne, Davy wants you.' He noticed Vinny and Carl mouthing something to him. 'Oh, sorry,' he cooed. 'I mean, Da-vid. David wants you.'

I saw Craig watching from the middle of the play-ground. He held out his hands as if to say *Sorry*. I smiled weakly; what could he have done?

'Did you hear me, Lianne?' called Webbo. 'David wants you.'

Lianne fixed him with a glare of contempt. She never did have any time for his antics.

'Oh, sorry I breathed,' hooted Webbo, before running across the yard, shoving and jostling Carl and Vinny as he went.

'You ought to keep away from those three,' advised Lianne. 'They're OK on their own, but once they're together they really get on my nerves.'

'Chance would be a fine thing,' I murmured.

'Did you want anything?' she asked.

'No, they were just trying to make me feel stupid.'

'You shouldn't let them, you know.'

'And how do I stop them?'

'Tell somebody,' said Lianne simply. 'Tell Clarkey.'

'I think he already knows,' I confided.

'Well then,' said Lianne. 'You've got no problem, have you?'

'That's all right for you to say.'

'Meaning?'

'You're a girl,' I explained.

'So what?'

'So you don't get bullied.'

'Who doesn't?' exclaimed Lianne. 'Girls are just as bad. Worse!'

I turned away. Craig was playing ollies with Sean Phelan.

'So why don't you tell Clarkey?' continued Lianne.

'Then what?' I snapped. 'I'd just get battered, wouldn't

I? Three to one. That's not very good odds, especially for a wimp.'

'Why do you let them call you that?' asked Lianne.

'Can't stop them, can I?' I replied.

Lianne shook her head. 'You never will if you don't do something.'

'Everybody's good at handing out advice,' I grumbled.

Lianne's face fell. 'Do you want me to go?'

'No,' I said hurriedly. 'Ignore me. I'm fed up, that's all.'

'I know how to cheer you up,' said Lianne.

'How?'

'Come to this dance thing with me.'

'You're joking!'

'I am not. I want to go, but I'm not going alone.'

'Well,' I said, 'I'm not going. It'll be all girls.'

'I don't see why.'

'But it's dancing! You don't get boys at dancing.'

'You enjoyed it this morning,' Lianne reminded me. 'Don't say you didn't. I saw your face. You felt the same way as me.'

'Well, I'm not going to the college,' I said. 'I've got better things to do.'

'Like what?'

Yes, like what? Sitting in front of the TV, listening to The Mouth screaming, worrying about my stupid brother getting himself squashed under a passing car.

Like what?

'Things,' I muttered.

'Things,' repeated Lianne impatiently. 'You'd love to go, I know you would. You're just scared of those three idiots, aren't you?'

'Oh, leave me alone, will you?'

'I'll leave you alone when you start to stick up for

yourself,' said Lianne. 'Now, are you coming to the dance class? My dad will run us.'

Webbo and Co. were drifting towards us, drawn by my obvious discomfort.

'I can't,' I answered in a voice which was almost a whine.

'Just because of them?' demanded Lianne. 'Davy, you *are* a wimp.'

'That's what we keep telling everybody,' said Webbo, nudging Carl.

'Drop dead!' yelled Lianne, shoving past him to rejoin her friends.

'Touchy, isn't she?' said Vinny, before following Carl and Webbo back across the yard to the railings on Bride Lane. I stared after them, full of helpless anger. If Lianne could tell them to drop dead, why not me? I shuffled over to the low wall between the Infant and Junior yards and stood alone, thoroughly disgusted with myself. Half an hour before I had been flying, now I lay with broken wings. What made it worse was knowing it was me who had chosen to fly into the wall.

CHAPTER TWELVE
Brothers

'Is that your kid?' asked Craig, reversing the car.

I didn't need to ask where to look. Colin was popping wheelies on the pavement by the main road.

'Yes,' I said. 'That's him, the big dope.'

'He might be a big dope, but he can handle that bike,' said Craig admiringly.

'I wish you could handle the car,' I grumbled. Craig had absent-mindedly run my pride and joy off the path and it had overturned on the rough ground. I picked it up and straightened the aerial. 'Now this time be careful.'

Craig gave me a sheepish grin and squeezed the handset, sending the car screeching off towards the bollards by the pensioners' bungalows. I took my eyes of him and turned my gaze on Colin.

'Watch this one, Ricky,' he shouted.

Ricky Scholes didn't even pretend to be interested. 'That's kids' stuff, Col. Let's see you play a real game.'

My stomach turned over. I knew Colin wouldn't be able to resist the challenge.

'It doesn't half go, this car,' said Craig.

I continued my surveillance of Colin.

'The car,' he repeated. 'It's great.'

'Yes,' I said. 'I know.'

'What are you looking at?' he asked.

'It's our Colin, he's playing Chicken.'

'Let's take a look,' said Craig excitedly.

'Oh, not you as well,' I groaned. 'Can't you see it's stupid?'

'Only if you do it yourself,' he replied. 'I like watching though.'

I raised my eyes to heaven. 'You're worse than them. I bet you'll be happy when somebody gets themselves killed.'

'What's got into you?' he asked. 'It's only a bit of fun. It's all right if you can handle a bike.'

'And if you can't?'

'Then don't do it.'

Craig was getting on my nerves. Everybody was. With Anna, it was chicken this and egg that. Mum and Gran were still pumping me about the bullies at every opportunity, and Colin was rapidly reaching the point of no return. Dad? Well, he just didn't seem to be the same any more.

'Here you are, Col,' said Ricky, pedalling to the top of the mound. 'Watch and learn.'

With that, Ricky plunged down the mound and across the road in front of a white delivery van. The driver pulled up and got out, but Ricky was already out of sight.

'Young idiot!' yelled the driver, as Ricky shouted abuse from one of the Closes.

'Did you see that fat get?' he asked, on returning to the group around the mound. 'What a divvy.'

Colin had gone very quiet and was hanging round on the edge of the group. I knew he wanted out, but he lacked the bottle to just jump on his bike and ride off.

'Your turn, Col,' announced Ricky, singling him out.

'No,' said Colin. 'I don't feel like it.'

'You mean you daren't,' said Ricky, needling him.

'Don't be soft,' said Colin. 'I just don't fancy it tonight.'

'Tell you what,' said Ricky. 'Seeing it's your first time, I'll go up to the bend and tell you when one's coming. It'll give you an extra couple of seconds.'

'Ricky . . .' began Colin, but Ricky had already set off for the corner.

'Keep an eye on the remote control,' I told Craig.

'Why, where are you going?'

'To stop Colin doing something stupid.' That was the idea, but it was easier said than done.

'You're not going to do it, are you?' I asked him.

'What are you doing here?' Colin shot back angrily.

'I said, are you going to do it?'

'Keep your nose out,' hissed Colin. 'You're showing me up in front of my mates.'

'Coming!' barked Ricky from the corner.

I clung desperately to Colin's arm but he shrugged me off and pedalled up the mound.

'Colin,' I screamed. 'Don't!'

He took no notice. In the same split second that I saw the black Escort come into view, Colin made his move. The Escort was taking the bend too fast and was riding the camber of the road. It was accelerating out of the bend and rocking slightly on its suspension. Everything came in machine-gun bursts, like the fast forward on a video.

There was the car, black and barely under control. its radio thumping, and Colin already beyond the point of no return but without Ricky's single-minded commitment. I saw Colin look up and cry out. It was all over in a second. A loud blast on the horn, a clatter of crashing bike, and Colin was sprawling in the gutter. The Escort had swerved and missed him by a hair's-breadth. Fright had made him fall. This time the driver didn't even stop. The kids were spilling on to the road, yelling and gesturing after him.

'You all right, Col?' I asked breathlessly as I reached him.

'Yes,' he said stubbornly, if a little shakily. 'How's the bike?'

'I think you've bent the frame,' I replied. 'You're just lucky you didn't end up under that car.'

'Dad will kill me,' said Colin. 'It's only two months old.'

'Colin,' I yelled. 'Just think yourself lucky you're still alive.'

'Oh, shut up you,' said Colin.

Ricky hadn't joined the others chasing the Escort. He stood alone at the top of the Mound. 'Nice one, Col,' he shouted. 'That's the closest yet. I didn't think you had the guts.'

To my amazement, Colin grinned. 'You try and beat it,' he called.

'I don't believe this', I cried.

'Davy,' said Colin, shaking his head. 'You're just like an old woman.'

I watched him wheel the bike on to the pavement. 'It'll mend,' he said, inspecting the damage.

'Colin!' bawled Ricky. 'Here we go again.'

I looked up to see him hurtling down the mound. I glimpsed the car out of the corner of my eye, and my heart sank. It was Dad's.

Ricky had left it too late this time. His mind was still on Colin's fall and he'd misjudged the distance. His head turned and the front wheel wobbled. He knew he couldn't make it. I heard him cry out about the same time the brakes screamed. Then came the crunch of the bike frame and the low groan of Ricky falling.

Dad leapt from the car. 'Dear God,' he breathed. 'Can you hear me, son?'

People were running from the bus stop across the road.

'Young fools,' said one.

'They've had one near miss already tonight,' added another, jerking his thumb. Dad's head turned at those words. He saw a boy and a twisted bike – Colin.

'Don't say "I told you so",' said Colin, in a dull, low voice.

'I wasn't going to,' I answered. I was too relieved that he'd escaped injury to rub salt in his wounds. He was lying on his bed, staring at the ceiling. I dare say I've seen people looking more worried – but I can't remember when.

'Any news about Ricky?' he asked.

'Dad's just been round to see Mrs Scholes,' I told him. 'Ricky's got a broken leg and he's covered in cuts and bruises. She reckons it looks a lot worse than it is. It's a clean fracture.'

'How's Dad?'

'Really shaken up,' I replied. 'I thought he was going to kill you when he realized you were involved.'

'So did I,' said Colin, raising himself up on one elbow. 'You were great, Davy.'

'Don't bother to thank me if you're going to do it again,' I warned.

'I may be stupid,' said Colin, 'but not that stupid. That could have been me under the car.' He walked over to the window. 'I wonder how long I'll be barred in for?'

'A few days,' I suggested. 'Just don't ask about going out again, that's all, or the old man will hit the roof again.'

'Do you think he would have hit me?' asked Colin. 'I mean, if you hadn't stood in the way.'

'I don't know,' I replied. I did. I'd seen it in Dad's eyes, a rage which was raw and complete. Fear, anger and guilt in one look. 'Just try to forget it.'

'I wish it was that easy,' said Colin. 'How do I face Mum and Dad again?'

'Don't ask me. That's your problem. I've got enough of my own.'

'Like what?'

'Not what. Who. Webster and his mates, they've been shoving me around.'

'Do you want me to sort them out for you?' asked Colin, brightening. Once a dope, always a dope.

'You sort yourself out,' I retorted. 'Getting my brother to hit one of them would do me a lot of good, wouldn't it?'

Colin grinned foolishly. It was funny, talking like this. You'd think I was the older brother. I was in control again, like when I was dancing. I'd been proved right, and Colin was asking me about things, *me*, his kid brother, the wimp. If I was so good at sorting his problems out, why couldn't I do it for myself?

There was a knock on the door. 'It's me.'

Dad's voice. Colin looked scared. 'Stay with me, Davy.'

I nodded.

'We need to talk,' said Dad, as he walked in. 'Off you go, Davy.'

'Colin wants me to stay.'

'I beg your pardon?'

I repeated it. To my great surprise, Dad burst out laughing. Colin gave me a startled stare.

'No, Davy,' said Dad. 'I won't hit him if that's what you're thinking. I was angry and frightened before – mostly frightened. I don't know, I feel as if some of this is my fault. I've been too busy with my own problems to ask how you were getting along. I've let the whole family down.'

Colin and I exchanged glances.

'Right now,' said Dad. 'I just want Colin to tell me why he did it.'

I edged closer to Colin.

'It's all right, Davy,' he said with a smile. 'I'll be OK on my own.'

As I reached the door, Dad slipped a hand round my neck and pulled me to him. It was a clumsy gesture, a bit embarrassing really, but I didn't mind at all. It told me what Dad could never have put into words; I mattered.

'Just stay the way you are, Davy lad,' he said in a voice which was thick and gruff. I think he was trying to control his tears.

I closed the door and walked downstairs. Stay the way you are! It was easy to say, but what on earth did it mean?

CHAPTER THIRTEEN
The Plot is Hatched

'Here's your Anna,' hissed Craig.

Sure enough, there she was, large as life and twice as noisy. She had the nursery nurse, Miss Nicholls, and her mate Rebecca in tow. I could sense the others turning in my direction, but kept my eyes fixed on the door. If there was one thing I was getting good at, it was avoiding eye contact. In one small classroom I had learned to avoid:

One – Clarkey. he still hadn't forgiven me for holding out on him over the bullying.

Two – Lianne. She had it in for me for refusing to go to the dance class with her.

Three – Webbo, Vinny and Carl. Well, I was still breathing, wasn't I?'

Four – Antonia Plang. I don't like cold rice pudding.

'Pencils down and close your books,' ordered Clarkey.

I did as I was told, and waited.

'That means everybody,' boomed Clarkey. 'Even you, Sean Phelan. It's the height of bad manners to carry on working when I've told you to stop.'

Typical. Clarkey spent all day trying to get Sean to work, then the moment he actually did something he was told off for not stopping! Funny creatures, these teachers.

'Now,' said Clarkey, darting his eyes around the tables,

daring anyone else to as much as open a book or fiddle with a pencil. 'I think the Reception children have something to show you, Miss Nicholls?'

'Thank you, Mr Clarke,' she said. 'Show them what you've brought in to show, girls.'

Anna held out a cardboard box perforated with holes.

'Tell everybody what we've been doing,' prompted Miss Nicholls.

'Well,' said Anna. 'On Tuesday we got some eggs and and we put them in a . . .' She looked up at Miss Nicholls for help.

'Incubator,' came the helpful answer.

'We put them in an ic . . .' Anna dried up and blushed. I could hear Webbo muttering something about all Woollybacks being thick.

'Incubator,' whispered Rebecca.

'We hatched them,' said Anna hurriedly, and she thrust the box forward.

Lianne led the sighs of 'Aw.' In the box were half a dozen tiny, fluffy yellow chicks.

'They hatched early this morning,' explained Rebecca. 'Just before we got to school.'

'And what sort of babies are they?' asked Clarkey, kneeling down. As a reception teacher he'd make a good airline pilot. It was the dumbest question I'd ever heard.

'Baby pigs,' giggled Sean.

'Chimps,' said Hanif. 'Baby chimps.'

'They're baby chickens,' said Anna, a bit puzzled by such a stupid question.

'Of course they are,' said Clarkey, still talking in that weird voice some adults save for young kids. He sounded like he'd overdosed on Blue Peter. 'I bet you're really pleased with them.'

Anna stared, Rebecca nodded and Miss Nicholls smiled.

'Well, Year Six,' said Clarkey. 'Let's give them a clap.'

I joined in the scattered applause, and caught sight of Webbo in the corner of my eye. He was nudging Vinny and there was something about the way he was staring at the chicks which made my heart sink. He wouldn't. Not even Webbo could sink that low. Or could he? That's when something snapped. I wasn't going to let them do this to our Anna. They could have a dig at me but they weren't going to hurt my little sister. I looked up at the clock. Ten to twelve. 'Craig,' I whispered, 'I think Webbo's up to something.'

'What's new?' he replied casually.

'No, I mean *really* up to something. Something rotten.'

Craig frowned.

'I mean—'

'Davy Watts,' thundered Clarkey. 'Have you finished?'

'No, Mr Clarke.'

'Then save the talk for the playground. I want to take this work in at the end of the session.'

Craig bent over his book.

'What was all that about Webbo?' he asked, as we closed our books at twelve o'clock.

I glanced to make sure Webbo wasn't listening. 'I think he's going to do something to Anna's chicks.'

'Don't be soft!'

'He is; I saw him looking at them.'

'We all looked at them,' said Craig. 'So what?'

'It's the way he did it,' I said. No wonder he didn't believe me. What proof did I have?

'Come on,' Craig continued, shaking his head. 'Let's have a game of ollies before dinner.'

I played a lousy game of ollies, or should I say lousier than usual. I lost two steelies and a blue moon.

'You're a pushover,' said Craig, pocketing his collection.

Of course I was. I only played the stupid game to hang on to the one mate I had.

'Where's Webbo?' I asked anxiously.

'I don't know. What's up?'

'I told you.'

'Oh,' sighed Craig. 'That again.'

'Well, where is he?' I repeated.

'Search me. You're getting really boring about this.'

I didn't care how boring I was. I scanned the playground. No Webbo, no Carl, no Vinny either. They were definitely up to something.

'Well, there's Carl,' said Craig.

'Where?'

'By the Infant gate.'

Carl was on his own, which was unusual, and he seemed to be looking for something.

'Where are you off to?' demanded Craig, as I made for the Infant yard.

I didn't answer. As I reached the dustbins, I caught sight of Vinny. He was actually in the Infant yard, peering round the corner.

'I told you,' I exclaimed. 'I told you they were up to something. They're keeping look-out for Webbo.'

Craig wasn't arguing now. 'You don't think he would do anything, do you?'

'I wouldn't put anything past him.' My mind was racing. 'Go and get somebody.'

'What?'

'You heard.'

'Who?'

'Who do you think? A dinner lady, a teacher, anybody.'

'What if he isn't doing anything?'

I sighed. 'Look at those two, will you?'

'But what do I say?' Craig's backbone had turned to pure jelly. And they called me a wimp!

'Anything,' I ordered. 'Just do it.'

I watched Craig take a couple of steps towards Mrs Leach, the new dinner lady, then stop.

'Go on,' I urged, then turned and walked straight past Carl. I couldn't wait for Craig, before I did something.

'Where do you think you're going?' asked Carl.

None of your business, is what I thought.

'None of your business,' is what I said.

Carl looked shocked. I took advantage of his surprise to jog across the Infant yard and past Vinny.

'Oi,' was all Vinny could manage, before I opened the Reception door and stepped in.

'What do you want?' demanded Webbo, as he turned round.

'I want to know what you're doing in here.'

'You what?' Webbo looked annoyed, but a bit frightened too. He was leaning over the tray of chicks.

'What are you doing?' I asked again.

'You've got ten seconds to get out of here or I'll burst you, Woolly.'

Try it, is what I thought.

'Try it,' is what I said.

I could really get to like this new me.

Now, I suppose what should have happened next goes something like this. Webbo sees the error of his ways, puts down the tray and he learns to respect me for what I am. Is that what happened? Not on your Nelly.

'Do you know you're one cheeky get?' he asked, and struck me in the face with his fist.

My face went numb. I hadn't felt anything like it since my last visit to the dentist.

'Now, shove off.'

'No.'

Webbo's eyes narrowed as he took a step forward. 'Say that again.'

'No.'

'You're asking for it.'

'Hit me if you want,' I said. 'Just leave the chicks alone.'

'What if I don't?'

'If you don't,' came a familiar voice, 'I'll take you straight to Mr Clarke and see what he has to say.'

Good old Craig. He must have brought the cavalry just in time.

'Miss Nicholls,' I exclaimed, as much in surprise as in relief.

'It's John, isn't it?' she said, looking Webbo in the eyes.

No reply.

'Are you supposed to be in here?'

No reply.

'Well?'

Without another word, Webbo turned on his heels and marched out.

'How's the nose?' asked Miss Nicholls.

I hadn't realized until then it was bleeding.

'I'm bleeding,' I said.

'Sit down,' she said, pinching the bridge of my nose.

It was about then that the Infants swept in from the hall. The first sitting for dinner had just finished. I ask you, some hero I'd make. Sitting with blood spots on my shirt and the nursery nurse holding me by the hooter. It wasn't quite the way I'd imagined it.

'Out you go,' ordered Miss Nicholls.

'What happened to you, Davy?' asked Anna.

I got hit on the nose, is what I thought.

'I god id ob de dose,' is what I said.

'Silly,' said Anna, skipping out into the yard.

Silly! I'm a hero, you little worm!

'There,' said Miss Nicholls. 'Don't blow it for a bit.'

'Thanks,' I said, 'for everything.'

'What was that boy up to?' she asked.

'Don't you know?'

'I think I do,' she replied. 'I'll tell Mrs Collins. Thanks, Davy.'

I walked into the hall and found Craig. He'd saved me a place and my lunch box was ready for me.

'I knew you wouldn't let me down,' I said, as I slid in next to him.

He continued munching his butty.

'I said thanks, Craig.'

Still no answer. The only sound was the clicking of his jaws.

'Craig, did you hear me?'

'I didn't tell,' he said quietly.

'What?'

'I didn't tell anybody,' he repeated. 'I was scared.'

'Didn't tell!' I gasped. 'So how did Miss Nicholls know we were there?'

Craig's jaws clicked rhythmically as I racked my brains. 'It must have been a coincidence,' I announced finally. 'If she hadn't turned up, I'd have been battered.'

'Sorry.'

'You should be.'

'Do you still want to sit with me?' he asked.

'Yes,' I replied with a grin. 'I still want to sit with you. All the wimps together.'

CHAPTER FOURTEEN

Testing Times

It was all the wimps together for rounders too, so I stuck close to Craig. If the ball came anywhere near us, he could go for it.

'Yes!' he roared with delight as Hanif caught Vinny low and to his left. 'They've no chance. Two rounders down and only two to bat.'

I wasn't so sure. I had this uncanny knack of snatching defeat from the jaws of victory. As Sean walked up to bat I could feel my heart sinking. It had just about reached my ankle when Sean struck the ball with the meat of the bat towards the fence bordering Bride Lane. Antonia Plang pursued it with all the speed cold rice pudding could muster, and promptly lost it in the long grass beyond the fence. By the time Lianne arrived to retrieve it, Sean had scampered home.

'Me and my big mouth,' groaned Craig.

No comment.

Webbo stepped up. Judging by the smirk on his face, he fancied himself as the hero of the moment. He got his chance, too; the ball was a real dolly and Webbo gave it all he had. I bit my lip. The idea of Webbo squaring the match was just too much.

'He's skied it!' yelled Craig. 'Mine.'

It wasn't his. The moment he set off after it, his trainers

skidded on the greasy turf and he ended up sprawling full
length.

'Catch it!' screamed Lianne, seeing me standing with
my mouth open.

'Catch it!' chorussed my team mates.

I grimaced. Hero time again. The ball was dropping
right into my hands. All I had to do was cup them and
wait.

I cupped, I waited, I failed. The ball didn't pop out this
time, it just fell straight through.

'Holes in them?' asked Craig.

'Must be,' I sighed.

'Did you do that on purpose?' demanded Lianne
furiously.

'What?'

'To avoid trouble,' she explained. 'Is that why you
dropped it?'

'It was a mistake,' I said hotly. 'I just dropped it, all
right?'

'Like you just bottled out over the dance lesson,' she
retorted. 'They've really got you on the run, haven't
they?'

On the run? She wouldn't say that if she knew how I'd
saved the chicks.

'They haven't!' I yelled.

'Prove it.'

I could hear Webbo laughing. 'Thanks, Woolly,' he
called. 'We'd never have got the draw without you.'

Very funny.

Prove it, eh? OK, I will.

'I'll go to the dance lesson,' I said bluntly.

'You're joking!' gasped Craig.

'Are you?' asked Lianne.

'No,' I said, 'I'll go.'

Lianne cocked her head. 'Really?'

'I'll go, I'll go. What do you want, my hand on the Bible or something? I'll go, I'll even be your partner.'

Lianne pulled tongues and walked away after her friends.

'Don't you dare bottle out,' she called.

'No chance,' I replied.

Craig was giving me a really funny look. 'You're going to do it, aren't you?'

'Yes.'

'You and Lianne Whalley? You want your head seeing to.'

'So do you,' I said with a grin. 'But I don't talk about it.'

'Cheeky get.'

The funny thing is, just when I thought Webbo would be making things really tough for me, he seemed to lose interest. Sure, he trotted out the usual stuff about wimps and woollybacks, but it was like water off a woolly's back. I didn't care. So he'd given me a bloody nose; what more could he do? I had his measure and he knew it. My problem hadn't been Webbo, but fear of Webbo. Now the fear was gone and only Webbo remained. Had I really been afraid of an idiot like that?

'Gran!' I exclaimed, as I reached the school gates with Anna. 'Where's Mum?'

'Wouldn't you like to know?' said Gran, with a mischievous grin.

'Oh, where is she?' asked Anna.

Gran just tapped the side of her nose. I hate it when people do that!

'Is it a secret?' asked Anna.

'Yes,' replied Gran, 'I suppose it is.'

'What is it? What is it?' squealed Anna, hopping from one foot to the other.

'You'll see soon enough.'

'Oh, Gra-an,' moaned Anna.

I saw Lianne pointing me out to her dad. 'We'll pick you up at six o'clock tomorrow,' she called. 'If you don't bottle out, that is.'

'Bottle out?' I said. 'No way.'

Lianne winked and jumped into the car beside her dad.

'Aye aye, Davy, who's that then?' asked Gran. 'A bit young for girlfriends, aren't you?'

'She's my partner,' I said, 'I'm going to dance lessons.'

'Dance?' said Gran.

'Dance?' giggled Anna.

'Dance,' I repeated simply, and stared them out, challenging them to say another word.

'It runs in the family, of course,' observed Gran. 'You should see me tango.'

'I'd rather not,' I replied.

'Cheeky thing,' said Gran.

'See you, Woolly,' shouted Webbo.

'Not if I see you first,' I answered coldly.

'That wasn't very nice,' said Gran.

'It wasn't meant to be.' Yes, I definitely liked this new me. Who knows? One of these days I might actually catch somebody out in rounders.

Anna spent the whole walk home pumping Gran about the secret but Gran was one old bird who wasn't going to sing. Even when Dad arrived home at a quarter to six, none of us was any the wiser.

'Where's Sandra, Mam?' he asked.

'That's what I want to know,' grumbled Colin. 'I want my tea.'

'It's a secret,' explained The Mouth.

Dad looked at me.

'It's a secret,' I repeated, enjoying Dad's puzzled expression.

'But she should be at work,' said Dad.

'She took tonight off,' said Gran. 'Somebody's covering for her.'

'Oh.'

That's when it happened. A car pulled up in front of the house, and I heard footsteps on the path. Before any of us could say a word, Gran flew to the door and flung it open.

'Well?' she asked, as Mum walked into the hall.

Mum hung her coat up.

'Well?' asked Gran again.

Mum shook her head slowly.

'Oh, you didn't?' groaned Gran.

'No,' said Mum with a broad smile, 'I didn't. I passed!'

'You passed. I knew you would.'

'Passed?' asked Dad. 'Passed . . .'

'Her driving test,' I interrupted. 'It's your driving test, isn't it?'

Mum nodded. 'My instructor said all the best drivers pass the second time round.'

'That's an old wives' tale,' grumbled Dad.

'You'd have to say that,' said Gran.

'What does that mean?' asked Colin, suddenly more interested in the conversation than his tea.

'Yes,' I said. 'What do you mean?'

Dad was staring at the floor.

'Is it a secret?' asked Anna.

'Oh, it's a secret all right, isn't it Ray?' asked Gran.

Dad wasn't happy.

'Tell them,' said Mum. 'I wish I'd known all those times he shouted at me about my driving.'

'Tell us what?' asked Colin.

'Only that your dad failed *twice*,' explained Gran, enjoying Dad's discomfort.

'You mean you only passed third time,' cried Colin.

Dad was grinning ruefully. He'd been rumbled!

'And he was scared stiff of driving lessons,' added Gran to rub salt in his wounds. 'He was on the toilet for an hour before he went out.'

'You chicken,' said Colin, giggling at Dad's embarrassment.

'Yes,' I added, digging Dad in the ribs. 'Chick . . .'

Colin joined me: 'Chick . . .'

Dad decided to join in the game, even if it was all at his expense. Smiling broadly, he gave chase throwing his holdall after us.

Slamming the door behind us we fled into the kitchen and roared at the top of our voices: 'CHICKEN!'